The
Papers
of
SHERLOCK
HOLMES

Volume II

by
DAVID MARCUM

Paperback ISBN 9781780924458
ePub ISBN 9781780924465
PDF ISBN 9781780924472

Published in the UK by MX Publishing
335 Princess Park Manor, Royal Drive,
London, N11 3GX
www.mxpublishing.co.uk
Cover design by www.staunch.com

For Rebecca and Dan,
who put up with it all,
and for my Mom, Dad, and Sister
who first encouraged it....

CONTENTS

How This Book Came To Be . . . .

As I related in the introduction to Volume I of this collection, there are two versions of how this book came to be written. The first version is that I, after having spent my thirties going back to school part-time in order to get a second college degree in Civil Engineering, became employed in said field in my early forties, only to be laid off during the recession of 2008. Having a lot of time on my hands, and a list of chores (sweetly labeled "Suggestions" by my wife) hanging over me, I thought "What did Conan Doyle do when he was sitting around waiting for work? Why, he wrote some Sherlock Holmes!" So, after a lifetime of collecting, reading, and studying literally thousands of narratives regarding my heroes, Holmes and Watson, in every conceivable form — novels, short stories, radio and television episodes, movies, comic books, scripts, and fan fiction, as edited by other people — I was able to fulfill a lifelong dream of adding my own efforts to the Great Watsonian Over-Soul. I sat down at the computer and let the stories flow. That's one version of what happened.

The other version is . . . *I found one of Watson's notebooks.*

It happened this way: During the time I was laid off, I went with my father to help clean out my aunt's house. She suffers from Alzheimer's and had been moved to a nursing home several years earlier. The place was a mess, and it had been an ongoing but irregular process to clean it.

On our final trip up there, we loaded up the last of what we wanted to save from the nearly empty building. My aunt had always been interested in genealogy and our family tree, and she had accumulated a vast amount of information, none of it too organized. My sister had acquired most of it, since it interested her too, and as far as I was concerned she could have it. As we finished cleaning the house, I saw one old pile of papers, photographs, and notebooks that had been missed during all the other trips. Grabbing them and throwing them into a box, we loaded up and departed.

1

Several weeks later, while sorting through the piles, I happened to go through those papers in order to see if they should be passed on to my sister. One of the items was an old, somewhat stained, school composition book, filled with faded and rather cramped writing. My aunt had been a schoolteacher, and I assumed that this was simply some long-ago assignment from one of her students. I flipped through it quickly, just to make sure it was useless before tossing it.

It was my subconscious that saved the book from the garbage. Years of searching for Sherlock Holmes stories has trained me to observe what others only see. I can scan numerous titles for words beginning with *S* and *H*, and often they seem to jump out at me, occasionally turning out to be something containing the words *Sherlock Holmes*. In this case, I saw on the rapidly flipping pages a few words that would probably not normally be included in an old student essay: "The Adventure of . . . ."

As any Holmes student can tell you, that electrifying combination of words often leads to a Holmes story. But why were they in an old handwritten notebook? Had someone felt the need to copy one of the original stories as an assignment for one of my aunt's classes? That seemed unlikely, and really a waste of time.

I started reading. And then I went cold. I've played The Game for a long time, but I was finally holding the real deal in my hands: *These were original Sherlock Holmes cases, handwritten by Watson.*

Of course, the next question was how did this notebook end up in my Aunt Wilma's papers? Only after reading more of the volume was the question answered, and that answer electrified me even further.

My great-grandmother on my father's side was named Rebecca Watson Marcum, daughter of James Watson. I was amused in my twenties when I finally connected that I had Watson blood in me. Later, in my thirties, I was even more amused when I first heard an episode of the Sherlock Holmes radio show, "The Case of the Very Best Butter" (from *The New Adventures of Sherlock Holmes* Radio Show, April 18, 1948) in

2

which Holmes tells Watson that he is distantly related to the Rathbone family. For you see, my mother's maiden name is Rathbone. At the time I first heard "The Very Best Butter," I just assumed that Holmes's statement about his connection to the Rathbone family was a tip-of-the-hat to Basil Rathbone, who had played Holmes for so long on both radio and in the movies. Little did I know . . . .

Further examination of the notebook from my aunt's house revealed that it contained nine of Holmes's investigations, each from different periods of his career. Six are more traditional narratives, and were included in Volume I. This volume contains the remaining three adventures. One of these was quite a bit longer than the others, and seems to answer several questions about Holmes's family. The two remaining stories involved a trip by Holmes and Watson to East Tennessee, where my family has lived for generations. It was on this trip that Holmes and Watson met my great-grandmother, Rebecca Watson Marcum, as well as her son (and my grandfather) Willie Marcum, and Willie's small daughter (and my aunt) Wilma, thus setting into motion the circumstances leading to Watson's notebook being found in my aunt's possessions. Although there is not much mystery to the first of these narratives, it was during this meeting that Holmes was able to fulfill an old vow.

It was also on that same trip to East Tennessee that Holmes and Watson met my other grandfather, Ray Rathbone, and became involved in a singular adventure that probably would have gone undetected except for Holmes and Watson's presence. (If it seems unlikely that Holmes and Watson would visit East Tennessee, and in fact tread the very ground where I now live, simply consider all the other journeys that they have made to the home locations of other editors of Watson's writings, such as their trips to Canada, as detailed by Canadian writers Ronald Weyman and Stephen Gaspar, and numerous trips to Minnesota, as edited by Larry Millett. I have no doubt that many British editors of Watson's notes have discovered that Holmes and Watson made visits to their own hometowns as well. I have no shame in discovering that Holmes and Watson came to my

3

hometown. If I haven't yet made it to England to walk where they walked, it is comforting to know that they came here, to walk where I walk.)

During that journey to my hometown, Holmes and Watson visited some of the same places that I see today, explored the locations where I went to college (both times), and amazingly, appear to have visited one of my former houses and to have lodged at the very farm where my current house was later built.

Included at the back of the notebook rescued from my aunt's house were two handwritten letters to my grandfather, Willie Marcum. One of these letters is written by Watson, and the other by Holmes himself. Watson's letter explains that he was in the process of expanding some of his notes into full-length narratives, as contained in the notebook, and that he wanted his distant relative Willie to have the record of the case in which Willie was involved, upon its completion by Watson. The other letter, from Holmes, explains how the entire notebook was sent to Willie, and the tragic reason why. Both letters are included as an epilogue to this book.

Apparently, the notebook and letters were sent to my grandfather, Willie, and upon his death, they must have been collected and saved by my Aunt Wilma, who probably did not recognize them for what they were. I wish that I could ask her if she had any memory of meeting my heroes, although she would have been a small child at the time. Sadly, my grandfather Willie Marcum died in 1968, and my grandfather Ray Rathbone in 1976, the year after I started my study and collection of items related to the Master. I will never know from their own lips anything about their participation in the adventures recorded by Watson in his notebook. Hopefully they would not mind that their grandson arranged to have the narratives published.

As I mentioned, Watson's old composition book was stained in places. I have had to make occasional guesses at a few of Watson's intentions and abbreviations, and I have Americanized the British spellings. Anything that appears to diverge from Watson's original narrative is my fault.

I wish to dedicate this volume with love to both my wife Rebecca, who has always been more than patient regarding my fascination with the world of Holmes and Watson, a persistent form of my second — or never-ending first — childhood, and my son Dan, who is the neatest guy that I know, and who always knows a good story. Thank you both for everything!

DAVID MARCUM
May 4th, 2013

(The 122nd Anniversary of the Reichenbach Incident)

The Affair of the Brother's Request

HOLMES AND WATSON IN TENNESSEE (PART I)

I have related elsewhere how Sherlock Holmes and I visited the United States in May and June of 1921, as we traveled from New York City to Johnson City, Tennessee, and over the Blue Ridge Mountains to Linville, North Carolina. There, Holmes and I found ourselves involved in a complicated affair relating to his long-standing feud with the Moriarty family.*

By the fourth of June, the matter had not been completely resolved. However, there was nothing we could do for several weeks but wait for events to unfold. Holmes and I spent a few additional days exploring the beautiful areas around Linville, including nearby Grandfather Mountain, and the picturesque towns of Blowing Rock and Boone. My third wife had passed away several months earlier, and I was in no hurry to return to England. I sensed that Holmes felt no pressing need to return, as well.

At some point during our explorations, I mentioned to Holmes a few of the details of a visit that I had made to America

---

* EDITOR'S NOTE: The exact details of Holmes and Watson's journey through Johnson City, Tennessee and Linville, North Carolina can be found in "Sherlock Holmes and the Brown Mountain Lights", edited by James McKay Morton. The narrative was originally published *Mountain Living* magazine in 1977-78, and subsequently on the internet in a slightly revised form at www.carolina.cc/sherlock.html. It was this narrative that provided additional proof of Holmes and Watson's travels in the southeastern United States during the lifetimes of my grandparents.

the previous December with my wife. At that time, I had followed up on some of the research I had been making into my own family tree, and had managed to trace a branch that had emigrated to the United States many years before, traveling down through Virginia and into the wilderness of northern Tennessee. Although I tried to be subtle about my wishes, in case Holmes did not wish to fall in with my plans, he immediately perceived what I hoped to do.

"I certainly have no objection whatsoever to returning over the mountains and visiting for awhile in Tennessee," he said. "In fact, I was going to suggest something along those lines myself in the next day or so, as I have some business there that I have put off for far too long."

Holmes asked me where my relatives lived. "I suppose one can use the term relatives only in the loosest sense," I replied. "Their branch of the Watson family left Scotland so long ago that one would have to examine many generations to determine the exact connection between myself and my American cousins. However, the branch of the line in question appears to have ended in a small town on the northern Tennessee border known as Oneida. I have not communicated with anyone there, and I have only one specific individual to try to contact. I'm not sure if she has married with some other family, or if the name has been absorbed or lost."

At the time of this conversation, Holmes and I were sitting on the porch of the Green Park Inn in Blowing Rock, which had been our base of operations during the past few days as we explored the local countryside. As I rocked in my chair, Holmes leaned forward and checked his handy United States atlas, laid open on his bony knees. He ran his finger along the page, tracing a route and murmuring to himself. Finally, he sat back in the chair and said "This is more than satisfactory, Watson," he said. "My business is not too far from your Oneida. Train travel to the place may be a nightmare, but if you are game, we shall leave tomorrow."

7

"Where is your destination, Holmes," I asked. "And what longstanding business could you possibly have in the wilds of Tennessee?"

"Ah, Watson, I'm sure you've never heard of where I need to go. It is a curious little village known as Rugby, located some miles southwest of Oneida. I fear a long carriage ride that day. And as for my business . . . I am going to fulfill a promise from long ago, made if I should ever find myself back in that part of the United States."

"Back in that part?" I asked. "You have been there before?"

"Yes, Watson, many years ago. But I will tell you the tale in a few days, after I have had a chance to refresh my mind on the circumstances, and when we are closer to Rugby. It was long ago, and I must confess that the details have become somewhat hazy."

We continued to sit on the porch as I thought about Holmes and his previous trip, unknown to me, to the American Southeast. I had known him for over forty years, and although we were both in our late sixties at this point, he still had the power to surprise me. There were so many parts of his past that I would probably never be told, in spite of the fact that in many ways we were as close as brothers. He was naturally secretive, he liked to withhold other facts just in case he could reveal them dramatically someday, and the nature of his work required that some things could never be told. I was simply grateful that, even after so many years, I would soon be finding out additional information about something that had taken place during Sherlock Holmes's travels.

The next morning, shown in my journal as the seventh of June, 1921, Holmes and I departed quite early to make certain that we did not miss our train. Slowly we wound our way over the mountains. The scenery was amazing, like nothing I had observed anywhere else in the world. I had seen the mountains of the Indian highlands and Afghanistan, as well as the Swiss Alps and other wonders of six continents. However, nothing could compare with the wildness around us. The ancient forests spilled down the mountains to shallow, fast streams and rivers.

Occasionally a tiny hamlet or grouping of cabins or farm buildings might appear, on a small plot cut back into the forest, but they were nothing compared to the thousands of square miles of old-growth forest and wildlife.

At times the train seemed to struggle as it pulled its tired way up along steep mountainside drop-offs. I questioned the wisdom of building a railroad in some of the locations where we traveled, and then realized that the builders had probably picked the easiest way, indicating that other routes would have been even worse. I simply tried to have faith in the railway and hope for the best.

The view never palled, in spite of hours of being surrounded by tall dark trees, so thick that one could not see much past those growing beside the tracks. We saw deer, too many to count, eating in the shade along the tracks. Most were visible in the morning, but the observations decreased dramatically toward the middle of the day. We saw a fair number of black bears, however, throughout the day. Both the deer and the bears appeared to have no fear of the train, simply pausing in whatever activity in which they were engaged as we passed, staring at us as we stared at them.

I have since read that the Appalachian Mountains are among the oldest in the world, and that their rounded heights are due to many more millennia of weathering than the younger Alps or the American Rockies. I know that the mountains over which we traveled contained some of the last remnants of the old forest that at one time covered a great deal of the entire North American continent, and that they were not as deserted or wild as they appeared to me that day. Settlers had moved all through those mountains, creating little communities and pockets of civilization connected throughout the wilderness. On that day, however, I found it easy to believe that, except for the train in which we rode, there were no other people within hundreds of miles. The mountains seemed to be saying that they were here before us, and they would be here long after we were gone.

The landscape gradually began to change as we descended on the Tennessee side of the slopes. Farms and towns became much more apparent, and the illusion I had felt while riding through the forest faded somewhat. By mid-afternoon, our train arrived back in Johnson City, where we had departed for Linville just days before.

As I waited on the bustling platform, looking at the nearby hills and breathing the clear air, Holmes arranged to find seats on the train bound south for Knoxville. I eavesdropped on several nearby conversations, enjoying the various local dialects in the same way that I did when traveling through different parts of the British Isles.

Holmes gestured toward me. As I joined him, he began quickly walking down the platform. "We are just in time to catch the Knoxville train," he said. "I was afraid that we were moving so slowly through the mountains that we would miss it, and have to stay here tonight."

Like all the trains I had seen in this part of the United States, the carriage did not have separate compartments, so we found seats within one that was only two-thirds full. After several minutes of maneuvering through the busy train yard, we reached an open landscape and picked up speed, heading south.

I was fascinated with the surroundings, but Holmes appeared lost in thought. Finally, he sank lower in his seat, made himself more comfortable, and began to doze. I, on the other hand, continued to look around me at the passing countryside. We were traveling south down a long, wide valley, with mountains in the far distance on both the east and west. Although we passed some wooded areas, none were as thick or old as those we had been through that morning in the mountains.

Most areas seemed to be devoted to agriculture, with many lonely houses perched in the middle of vast fields, within sight of the train tracks, but miles from their nearest neighbors.

I recalled Holmes once commenting on lonely country houses, and the horror that they gave him. "You look at these scattered houses, and you are impressed by their beauty," he had said. "I look at them, and the only thought which comes to me is a feeling of their isolation, and of the impunity with which crime may be committed there."

I had questioned how he could feel that way. He replied, "They always fill me with a certain horror. It is my belief, Watson, founded upon my experience, that the lowest and vilest alleys in London do not present a more dreadful record of sin than does the smiling and beautiful countryside."

"You horrify me!" I had cried.

He had explained that in town, everyone lived so closely that no vile deed could go unknown or unpunished. In the country, however, there were no nearby neighbors to know the crimes that happened there.

"Think of the deeds of hellish cruelty," he had said, "the hidden wickedness which may go on, year in, year out, in such places, and none the wiser."

Looking at the lonely houses, now in shadows from the setting sun, I was glad that Holmes was asleep. Although I knew that he was probably right, I preferred to look at them with optimism, and try to see their beauty, rather than their potential for evil.

We arrived in Knoxville late that evening. As we stepped out of the ornate station, we could smell the nearby stockyards and meat processing plants, along with a smell that I later identified as roasting coffee. On the horizon was a glow which resembled a fire, but I knew that it was simply electric lighting, shining from the businesses along the city's main thoroughfare. We engaged a cab, who drove us several blocks before depositing us at a small hotel, located beside the bluffs dropping to the nearby Tennessee River.

We checked into the hotel, and after freshening ourselves, went out onto the street, where we walked for an hour or so before finding a restaurant. We ate a quiet meal, and then set off to the west, where we found the sprawling grounds of the University of Tennessee. Compared to the ancient buildings of Oxford and Cambridge, the school appeared to be an upstart child. We entered some of the buildings, including Estabrook Hall, which were left open for late studies by the students. After an hour or so we returned to our hotel rooms, planning to make an early start in the morning.

11

The next day, Holmes and I were at the train station with time to spare, making sure we understood the convoluted route we would need to take to reach Oneida. After hearing the details of our journey, I began to question why I had not simply opted for a return to England by way of New York. Perhaps a few days in America's most successful city would have been more enjoyable than moving west into the remote and rugged poverty-stricken areas of the country. However, I recalled that Holmes had business there as well, and if I had not initially suggested a trip to Tennessee, he probably would have.

Our train left promptly, an odd mixture of passenger and freight cars. I had not thought of Knoxville as a particularly prosperous city, although I knew it was probably the largest metropolis in that part of the world. However, its citizens had looked considerably wealthy in retrospect as compared to the individuals currently sharing our carriage. Although a few of the men, such as Holmes and myself, were dressed in suits, most were dressed in work clothes, clean but much worn and well used. The few women traveling on the train wore plain dresses, augmented by bonnets, often the only color shown in their outfits.

As I pondered our fellow traveling companions, I thought of what I knew about the area to which we traveled. Based on my researches of the previous year, I had learned that the area was still considered somewhat wild, lying toward the middle of the state along the Tennessee-Kentucky border. It was a land of harsh, dramatic wilderness, but in a different sense from that which we had crossed in the mountains the previous day. The geographic feature to which we journeyed was on the edge of Tennessee's central Plateau region, a vast area which straddles the center of the state like a table. The western side of the state drops from the plateau toward the rich fertile lands along the Mississippi River. On the eastern side was the wide Tennessee River valley, down which we had partially traveled the previous day from Johnson City to Knoxville. Of course, other smaller mountain ranges bounded different portions of this valley as well, but essentially the valley lay between the plateau and the Appalachian Mountains on the state's far eastern border.

The plateau itself existed due to a variety of geologic causes. I had learned that the area near Oneida was quite unique in terms of its various natural wonders, such as stone arches and towering sandstone bluffs. In some way they reminded one of America's southwest, except that there the natural wonders were exposed in a desert-like setting, while I had read that the eastern Tennessee Plateau was still covered in old forest, hiding the geologic formations from view until one was almost on top of them and only if one knew where to look.

The state's capital, Nashville, lay to the southwest of our destination, far beyond the initial rise onto the plateau that we were now traversing.

As we traveled northwest, the land became more mountainous, folding on itself. We rode along the low-lands, beside streams and rivers and through dry valleys, our view of the sky limited to the open space between the tops of tall peaks.

After several hours, the people in the carriage began to shift restlessly and rearrange their belongings. I deduced that they were aware of our impending arrival. Holmes, who had been silent through the entire journey, seemed to notice as well, and sat higher in his seat. I wondered at his silence. I considered that perhaps he was still thinking of our unfinished business in Linville, or more probably that he was considering his task in the mysterious Rugby, where we would visit after finding my distant relations. I could tell that something about the idea of going to Rugby saddened him, but I knew better than to ask, and that he would tell me only when or if he was ready.

The train pulled into a station which lay next to a wide tangle of tracks, far more than I would have suspected for a remote town such as Oneida. Many of the tracks had rows of rail cars sitting idly, being connected in some random manner in order that they might be taken elsewhere. Our train seemed to be pulling the only passenger cars in sight, as all the others were loaded with heaping mounds of black coal or long trees, stripped of their branches, bound for the lumber mills.

13

As we stood next to the station, the conductor yelled, "All aboard! All aboard for Jamestown!" The last of the passengers not already loaded scurried to the train, and within moments, the great mechanical beast had gone, continuing down the tracks away from the direction of Knoxville.

There were no cabs outside the station, but as the town did not seem to be very large at all, we asked a man at the ticket window for directions to a hotel. He looked at us for a long silent moment, no doubt considering our British accents, before directing us down a dirt street and around the corner of some buildings in the distance.

Holmes and I picked up our meager bags and started down the dusty lane. Luckily we had always traveled light, and carrying the bags was no great burden. As we moved closer to the cluster of buildings, I could see that they were actually the back of a row of structures that stood side-by-side up a paved roadway. A similar group of buildings was facing them across the street. In the distance were some houses, located on dirt side roads, each standing under large shade trees.

As we stepped onto the main street, and apparently the only paved street, of Oneida, we were watched by the natives with expressionless faces. All were dressed as the people on the train, the women in plain dresses, the men in worn work clothes. Some of the men were obviously coal miners, while others were farmers. Only the business owners and shop keepers were dressed in suits, although these were quite worn as well.

I was struck by the obvious poverty of the area. I knew that the town subsisted on the local coal mines and timber industry, as evidenced by the products loaded on the train cars in the rail yard. I was greatly reminded of towns in Scotland and Wales, where Holmes and I had traveled during several of his investigations. The people there had the same look, a lean pride and suspicion of outsiders. It was no surprise that I was reminded of those British towns and villages, as most of the people in this area were descended from Scottish, Irish, and Welsh immigrants. That, combined with the fact that coal mining towns have the same look and feel to them, whether in Wales or eastern Tennessee, and it was no wonder that it felt familiar.

We found a small hotel where we were able to obtain two rooms. I sensed that the rate charged to us was perhaps more than the manager usually asked, because we were obviously from somewhere else, but it was still cheaper than our rooms had been in Knoxville, so we made no complaint. After getting settled, we made our way to a nearby restaurant, where we ordered a late lunch.

I was intrigued by an item on the menu which I had seen elsewhere during a previous trip to the United States. It was identified as country ham, I suppose in contrast to city ham, which uses a different curing process. The country ham was very salty, thinly sliced, and fried tough in its own grease. However, the flavor was wonderful, and went very nicely with the local vegetables, green beans, potatoes, and turnip greens, as well as homemade bread. Holmes made do with a bowl of hearty stew, and bread as well.

Following a dessert of some sort of apple and dough confection, I leaned back quite satisfied, while Holmes glanced idly about the room. "Well, Watson," he said, "how do you wish to proceed in finding your distant relations?"

I glanced at the waiter, heading toward our table. "I suppose the best way to start is simply to ask." As the waiter arrived, I said, "We are looking for a lady that I believe lives here in town or somewhere nearby, and I wonder if you might know her. Rebecca Watson?"

The waiter said nothing for a moment, and then replied, "Why do you want to talk to her?"

"I am a distant relative," I said. "A very distant relative, and while I am passing through this area, I thought I would like to introduce myself to her."

The waiter thought for a moment, and finally seemed to decide that I passed some sort of test. "She lives here in town at times, and out at their home place at No Business on the Big South Fork at others. And she isn't a Watson anymore, either.

15

She's been married for years to a man named John Sherman Marcum."

Before I could ask where the picturesque area known as "No Business" was located, the waiter added, "But some of her sons live here in town. One of them works at the lumber mill, just on the other side of the train yard, not far from here. Willie Marcum. He should be there now."

Thanking the waiter, we paid our bill and departed. As we walked back down the humble street toward the train tracks, I thanked Holmes again for accompanying me on this journey.

"It is no bother, Watson. It is always a pleasure to see new parts of the world, and to observe that no matter how differently people live, in what circumstances or locations or state of wealth or poverty, they are still essentially the same, wherever one looks. And in any event," he continued, "I am still expecting your company when I complete my errand in this part of the world, at nearby Rugby."

After crossing through the rail yard, stepping gingerly over each parallel track, we reached the far side, where we found ourselves at the lumber mill. The whine of saws became louder with each approaching step, and the smell of freshly cut wood filled the air. We began to walk through small drifts of sawdust and strings of sawn bark.

Identifying the office, we entered and asked to speak to Willie Marcum. The man there did not question our business, but simply told us to wait a minute while he stepped outside. In no time, he returned with a tall man in his late twenties, his thin hair cut rather short but unkempt and waving in the slight breeze. He was wearing overalls, and sawdust was sticking to his clothing up and down his body.

In appearance, he somewhat physically resembled a younger version of Holmes. However, his facial expression was one of open friendliness, whereas Holmes, in contrast, had always maintained the watchful look of a predatory bird.

"Mr. Marcum," I said, "My name is Dr. John H. Watson, and this is my friend, Sherlock Holmes."

Mr. Marcum stuck out his hand in my direction, but his glance turned sharply toward Holmes at the mention of my friend's name. After shaking my hand, he shook Holmes's, whereupon he said, "You're kidding, right? Sherlock Holmes? I read about you in some books. I thought you were a made-up story."

Through the years, as my writings had become increasingly well known, this experience had happened more and more often. Holmes had managed to learn to respond politely when this type of thing occurred, but I knew that he had never come to appreciate the attention he had received from my published narratives.

"It is nice to meet you, Mr. Marcum," he said. "I am afraid that Dr. Watson's stories have given many people the impression that I am a 'made-up story.' However, I assure you that I am, in fact, a real person."

Mr. Marcum grinned and looked at the two of us. "I can see that. And call me Willie. It's short for William. What can I do for you two?"

I explained that I had been to the United States the previous year, and during that time I had researched some of my own family background, tracing various offshoots of the Watson family that had come to America from Scotland. "One linear relationship seems to have passed through Virginia and Kentucky into this area. Your mother is the most direct descendent of that branch that I can identify, and as Holmes and I were journeying through this part of the country, I wished to make a detour and possibly meet her."

"Well, I think she'd enjoy that very much," said Willie. "But she doesn't live here in town right now. The family has land here in Oneida, quite a bit of it actually, due to my father's foresight. My brothers and I have divided it and are farming it, but my parents spend time here and also a ways out in the woods, where all of us boys and my sisters were raised. Right now the family is out there, getting some things cleaned up after the place sat empty last winter."

"The waiter in town who told us how to find you said it was a place called 'No Business'."

"That's right," Willie replied. "I've been planning to go out there soon myself to help out. What I can do is leave today, if that's agreeable with you, and take you both with me."

"Why, certainly," I replied.

"Well, let me just tell my boss that I'm going, and we'll be on our way."

He was back in a moment, and said he was ready to go. "I hope you don't mind walking some, but I live a mile or two away, and we'll need to go by my house to get my truck. The saw mill is so close that I usually just walk back and forth every day."

Holmes and I assured him that it would not be a problem, and we headed back across the tracks and into town. On several occasions we stepped to the side of the road as horse-drawn vehicles went by. Much more rarely, we were passed by automobiles, or occasionally trucks, as the Americans called them, carrying lumber.

As we neared the hotel, Willie asked if our things were there. When we said yes, he replied, "You might as well check out and bring it all with you. By the time we get to my parents' place, it will be too late to come back tonight, and anyway, mother will insist that you stay overnight. It won't be as nice as the hotel, though. I hope you won't mind."

We assured him that we did not, and we entered the hotel. We were soon checked out, to the relative displeasure of the man behind the desk, and resumed our walk down the street. Within the lengths of a few buildings we had left the main part of town behind. We continued on out the dirt road, passing several nice homes, before bearing left onto a smaller lane. Around us were tilled fields, crossed by small brooks, and bordered by distant woods. "Almost there," Willie said, smiling.

We could see a white frame two-story house, wrapped on two sides by a wide porch, in our path. Behind it was a large barn. Near the barn was parked an old truck and a hay rake. Before we got too close to the house, the door opened and a woman stepped out and watched us approach. She was very pregnant, and I could see that she would deliver within just a few weeks. A young boy, six or seven years old, stood beside her, while a girl of about three years stood behind her, peeking from behind the woman's skirts.

As we reached the porch, the woman looked at us, and then said to Willie, rather sternly, "You're home early."

Willie nodded and said, "Ola, I want you to meet some people. These men are Mr. Sherlock Holmes, and Dr. John Watson, all the way from England. Gentlemen, this is my wife, Ola, my son Howard, and my daughter, Wilma. The doctor is distant kin to my mother, and I am going to take them out to the home place tonight to meet her."

Willie's wife greeted us politely, but I could see that she was not pleased that he was going to be leaving. "Will you be staying out there tonight as well?" Willie said yes, and she turned to us. "Could I fix you something to eat before you go? I've got some dinner left on the stove."

Holmes and I politely declined, explaining that we had only recently had lunch. Willie left us and walked to a nearby barn, where he was soon involved in starting the balky truck. Holmes glanced around the farm, his gaze lingering on a large walnut tree in the front yard. "You have a lovely place here," he said. "Are you from this area as well?"

"Yes," replied Ola. "I grew up right over the hill there. I was a Smith, and my father owns a small store."

The girl, Wilma, had sat on the porch floor and begun to play with some small broken bits of toys. Holmes gestured to the road near the house, which at that point was somewhat sunken between two high banks on either side. "That road must have been here quite a while to have been worn down so," he said. "I had not realized that Oneida had been settled for so long."

Ola glanced at the road. "I don't know how long that road has been there, but they say that General Burnside and his army marched on it during the Civil War. In fact, the troops camped right here on this land during the march. Although they were from the North, they were welcomed here, you know. When

19

Tennessee seceded from the Union to join the South, the town of Oneida and Scott County, where we are located, remained loyal to the North and seceded from Tennessee. As far as I know, we've never officially been put back into Tennessee, although it doesn't seem to matter to anyone now.

"This area was settled for who knows how much earlier, though, by Indians, although there's none left around here now. There are many places around here where you can find Indian bones and pieces of pots and arrowheads. There's a great rock sticking out of the ground within walking distance of here that has something of a cave beneath it. Everyone knows you can find old bones under the Indian Rock.

"And that field right over there," she said, pointing behind us. "We plow it every spring, and I can't tell you the number of arrowheads that turn up in the dirt. We have buckets full of them. I don't know what happened, whether there was a village there or a great battle, but somehow all those things were left behind in that field."

At that point, Willie drove up with the truck, and we took our leave from his wife. "Is it all right to leave your wife so close to her term?" I asked.

Willie nodded. "She's got kin staying with us. I'm just in the way. In any case, I'll be back before anything happens." He turned the vehicle, and started out in a westerly direction. "Sorry the trucks's not more comfortable," he said. "But if we went by wagon it would take until tomorrow to get there. I actually had one of those new automobiles, once. Ola and I managed to get it right after we got married. We drove it into town, the first one that was ever driven into Oneida. It was a rainy day, and the thing sank into the mud on Main Street, up past the tires. It was very embarrassing, but pretty funny, too."

We drove on past some farms before entering the woods again. "All this belongs to my family," he gestured, pointing left and right. "We used to have much more. My grandfather owned most of the land where the town is, but we've been selling it off over the years." The creaking of the truck's springs and the occasional grind of gears or a racing motor could not hide the

20

sounds of the numerous birds in the trees surrounding us. Holmes spent some of the time questioning Willie about the Indian artifacts and settlements mentioned by Willie's wife, but Willie had nothing further to add.

Suddenly, I interrupted when a question occurred to me. "What can you tell me about Rugby?" I said. "Are we close to it?"

"Rugby is about ten or fifteen miles on the far side of No Business, through some fairly rugged woods. It's a pretty rough ride. Why do you want to know about Rugby?"

I looked at Holmes, to see if he had any objection to my revealing the reason behind my question, or if the matter was some sort of secret. He showed no reaction. "After we meet your mother," I said, "Holmes has said he would like to go to Rugby. However, I've never heard of the place, and did not know exactly what it was. The name sounds British," I added. "There is a town in England of that name."

"I suppose I can take you there tomorrow," Willie said, "after we leave my parents' place. Then I can bring you back to Oneida, or take you on down to Rockwood, where you can catch a train to wherever you want to go. But as to Rugby, well, there isn't much there anymore. Although I hear that it was something special, once."

"You said you'd been there before, Holmes," I said. "Do you know anything of the place?"

Holmes's gaze, which had seemed distant and unfocused, sharpened, and he said, "Yes, I know some of the history of Rugby. Please feel free, Willie, to add in anything you might recall."

Holmes took another moment to focus his thoughts, and then began.

"Rugby was a community founded in about 1880 by Thomas Hughes, the British author — "

" — of *Tom Brown's Schooldays*," I interrupted. "I enjoyed it when I was much younger."

"As you say," agreed Holmes. "He named the town after Rugby in Warwickshire, where he had attended school, and which I believe served as the setting for his book.

"Hughes developed the idea that he wanted to build a perfect community, an experiment in cooperative effort with a strongly agricultural atmosphere. He recruited the younger sons of the English gentry, who had rather limited prospects if they chose to remain in England."

"Why limited?" asked Willie.

"In England," I answered, "there is an accepted system among the rich and noble classes known as *primogeniture*. Under this arrangement, the eldest son in a family inherits the property, the wealth, and the title should there be one. Often properties and estates are entailed, so that the eldest male heir has use of them through his lifetime, but he cannot sell them or pass them on as he might like. After his death, the next eldest male heir inherits the entailment.

"For younger sons in this system, there is usually very little money or property left over. They can live off their elder's charity, for as long as that lasts, and if anyone is willing to provide it. Or they can seek employment. There are very few socially acceptable jobs for younger sons. In many cases, it is assumed that younger sons will enter the military or government service, or will undertake a diplomatic post at some location in the Empire."

"I see," said Willie. "And these younger sons were the men that Mr. Hughes recruited to come live and work in Rugby?"

"Yes," said Holmes. "The idea of traveling to an area far from England and creating something of a 'New Jerusalem' in the wilderness was very appealing to these young men, the ones who did not want to or who were not suited to enter the military or government employ.

"Hughes and his new disciples came to Rugby, which had been purchased earlier by Hughes due to its proximity to a newly-built rail line nearby. They set to work, many of the young men doing that type of labor for the first time. They worked hard, and learned from their many mistakes. Soon a

22

number of buildings were constructed on the site. From my research at the time, I believe that in the first few years, the early 1880's, there were over seventy structures built, and over three hundred residents in the growing community.

"The young men, all of whom had been well-educated while growing up in England, attempted to bring their culture and society with them. By day they would work in the fields, tending their crops, and making repairs to their houses and community buildings. At night, they would have meetings of drama clubs and literary societies and numerous sporting teams. Within a few years, a fine inn had sprung up, a large well-stocked library had been built, and regular train service was connecting the town to the outside world, providing a means of obtaining other valuable goods and services.

"Of course, trying to build a paradise on earth is always doomed to failure. In the early years of the colony, a typhoid epidemic swept through the citizens. Word of this reached England, causing a decrease in confidence in Hughes's planned community. Later, in the mid-1880's, the inn, which had been the center of the community's activities and cultural efforts, burned to the ground. As time went on, Hughes himself began to spend less and less time in Rugby, possibly due to the fact that his family, which had initially lived there with him, began to absent itself more and more, eventually staying there only one month out of each year.

"Hughes continued to pour much of his own money into the colony, but it continued its downward slide into failure. Hughes died in the mid-1890's, a few years after I visited. By about 1900, the official colony was at an end, although I understand some people, descendents of the original settlers, continue to live there."

Holmes looked at Willie. "Is that essentially correct?"

Willie replied, "I suppose so, Mr. Holmes, but actually you know more about the place than I ever did, and I grew up near it. There are some people still living there, but they have always tended to keep to themselves, and now I guess I understand why a little better.

"I guess we will go over there tomorrow," he continued. "I would have liked to have seen the place in its heyday. You say you were there in the nineties?"

"In 1893," Holmes replied.

"The year I was born," interjected Willie.

Holmes nodded. "I was presumed dead for several years during that time, as you may have read."

"I read how you came back, too," said Willie with a grin. "Back when I thought you weren't real."

"Yes," said Holmes. "During those three years, I carried out a number of activities for my brother, working for the British government, in various locations in Asia, Europe, and North America. I traveled under a variety of aliases, and for a time, I lived in New York City. I think I may have referred to those times in the past, haven't I, Watson?"

I nodded, and he continued. "During the time I was in New York, I was notified that one of my great enemies, Colonel Sebastian Moran, might possibly be in that city as well, hunting me. In order to verify or disprove this, I surfaced and traveled quite openly from New York to Florida, taking care of several small matters of business along the way. Of course, I was constantly on the alert to see if I was being stalked.

"As my business in Florida neared completion, I notified Mycroft, who said he had a task for me in New Orleans. I went west for a short period of time. While still traveling there, Mycroft arranged for information to be sent ahead of me to New Orleans about Rugby and a small task he needed for me to accomplish there. I then passed through this part of Tennessee on my way back to New York."

"But what was the task?" I asked. "Why would your brother, whom you have said sometimes *was* the British government, need you to travel to this remote location?"

"Ah, Watson, that is a part of the story that I will tell you tomorrow, when we are on our way to Rugby."

The sun was setting as we finally reached the Marcum cabin. We had journeyed through the ancient forests, occasionally lurching as the truck was driven through narrow rock-choked streams, and once across a shallow riverbed. The muddy water came rather high on the wheels, and seemed as if it were threatening to overtop the sides of the vehicle as well on one or two occasions. However, it probably looked much worse to me than it actually was. "This is the Big South Fork," Willie said, calmly turning the wheel as the truck pulled us onward, seemingly oblivious to the water surging around its wheels and the uncertain footing in the hidden rocky river bottom. "The Big South Fork of the Cumberland River. We're lucky it's low right now. I would have had to go the long way around otherwise."

"Lucky indeed," I muttered, as water splashed over the side of the door, drenching my face.

We had no other mishaps on the river, however, and we were soon at the cabin, located in the bottom of a gorge along the river bank. As we neared our destination, I saw countless other homes nearby, and realized with surprise that this area was much more heavily populated area than I had expected. "Welcome to 'No Business,' " said Willie. "I guess they call it that because nobody has any business living way out here."

I had smelled wood smoke hanging in the air for quite a while before we arrived. Finally we rounded a bend and saw the Marcum cabin in the distance. At the side of the river nearby was a great round rock, probably twelve to fifteen feet around, squatting along the shore. Tied beside it was a small boat. My attention was drawn back to the cabin as a series of barks arose, coming from a group of lean-looking dogs rising to their feet near the door.

An older man and woman stepped from out of the cabin. In a moment they were joined by several young men and women, Willie's younger brothers and sisters, I assumed, from their similar physical features. The entire family had the look I had seen on a variety of people since arriving in this area. Obviously most of the people in these parts were of Scots-Irish descent. They were so similar to those that I had met in the small towns and villages of England. As I watched, more of the family appeared from various buildings around the main house. They waited silently as we arrived.

Willie hopped down lightly, while Holmes and I descended more cautiously. "Mother? Father?" Willie said. "I have brought someone who would like to meet you." Willie then introduced us, again explaining that we were from England. His father, a tall older man, stooped and wearing a large mustache, stepped up and gravely shook our hands, while his wife and children simply nodded. "Dr. Watson here has been tracing his family tree, and he has found that we are distant relations, Mother."

I had noticed an added interest when my name was mentioned. When Willie finished explaining my purpose, the small woman stepped forward, smiling for the first time. She was wearing a plain cotton dress, covered with a flour-specked apron. Her graying hair was pulled back in a bun, and her finely drawn features showed a beauty and grace that was unexpected to me in that wilderness. However, she reflected the hard life where she had lived, and looked older than she probably was.

"Welcome to our home, cousin," said Rebecca Watson Marcum. She took my hand, smiled also at Holmes, and pulled me toward the door. "You're just in time to eat."

We went into the log and plank building, very clean and tidy, and surprisingly well lit considering the small windows. The odor of kerosene was immediately noticeable from the numerous lanterns hung about the room, but it was not unpleasant. Mixed with it was the smell of vegetables and heat from the stove.

We crowded around the table, and the room began to fill with good-natured conversation as the brothers and sisters started to ask Willie of news from town and the farther world. We began to pass the dishes around, and both Holmes and I took generous helpings of the pork loin, green beans, potatoes, and the corn meal bread with fresh butter. Soon both Holmes and I were answering questions about life in England and our visit to the United States.

Willie explained that Holmes was a famous detective, and he told one of his brothers to go upstairs to retrieve a book, apparently originally owned by Willie and now left for the younger men. In a moment, everyone was eagerly passing around one of the published collections of Holmes's cases,

26

amazed that we were actually visiting in their home, and commenting that the illustrations did not much look like Holmes. I pointed out that the American illustrator had unfortunately based his drawings of Holmes on the likeness of a popular actor, while the British illustrator had been much more accurate in his portrayal of his subject.

Holmes took all of the attention in stride, responding good-naturedly to questions, and making a few simple deductions about the brothers and sisters, to the delight of all at the table. The meal passed far too quickly, and I tried to treasure every minute of it.

Later, Holmes and I sat with Mr. and Mrs. Marcum, and Willie, while the others went about their business. Mrs. Marcum and I spent a while looking through her old and fragile family Bible, tracing dates and relationships back to our common ancestor. I had brought some of my own documents with me, and we compared our information. Mine was surprisingly consistent with what was written in the Bible, and I could tell that Mrs. Marcum was glad to learn some about her family's earlier history in Scotland and England before her branch had emigrated to America.

I was aware that Holmes was talking with Willie and Mr. Marcum about various matters, including the description of the geology of the local area, with its dramatic bluffs, caves, and sandstone arches towering over the ground below. Willie offered to take us by one or two of the sites on the way to Rugby the next day, saying that it would not be too far out of the way. I heard Holmes asking a few questions about Rugby, but neither Willie nor Mr. Marcum had any additional information to offer.

That night, we were offered Mr. and Mrs. Marcum's bed, and when we wouldn't hear of it, they tried to turn out their children and give us their upstairs loft. Finally we convinced them that sleeping in the clean straw in the barn loft would suit us down to the ground, and, wrapped in warm blankets, we fell asleep to the sound of a soft wind and the distant chuckling of the river.

We were up early the next morning, finding that Mrs. Marcum had been up even earlier, making biscuits, which we ate with more of the fine country ham, preserves, and local honey. After saying our goodbyes, Willie drove us away in his truck. I turned and waved until a bend in the dirt road put them out of sight. Settling back in my seat, I was very glad that we had come here. My new world relatives, however distant, were fine people, and I would not have missed this for the world. I was saddened when I realized that I would not be able to share my experiences with my recently deceased wife, who had participated so often in the research into my family's history.

Willie drove through a meandering series of narrow roadways, up and down hills, along ridges, and down in small valleys opening onto flat lands before rising again. He seemed to know exactly where he was going. Occasionally through the trees, I could see distant cliffs, rising far over the valley, their vertical walls worn smooth by countless eons of wind and rain. Sometimes caves seemed to be visible high on the inaccessible cliff faces, but it may have been a trick of the shadows.

Once we stopped at a cabin so Willie could pass on a message from town to the occupants. It was a rude little place, with low ceilings and small rooms that could only be reached from the outside, with no internal access between rooms. It seemed as if the place were more of a barn than a home for the poor little family that lived there. Nearby was a small stream that Willie identified as Charit Creek. I knew that if the creek flooded, portions of the home would be underwater.

Eventually we departed, the children staring at us in silence until we were out of sight. I realized that our visit was probably the most exciting thing that had happened there in weeks. Gradually we were pulled higher until we seemed to be out of the valleys and onto a small plateau. A short distance away, suddenly visible, was a pair of twin arches, giant stone behemoths carved by uncountable years of water and wind.

Willie stopped beside them and we all stiffly climbed down, sore from sitting for so long, and also from constantly moving to retain our balance in the ever-shifting truck. We walked up to the arches, dwarfed by their size. Standing under the larger arch, I looked up, realizing that the inner roof was so far above me that I could not make out any details in the stone. The floor of the arch was shaded and sandy, and filled with large boulders, some as big as a room. I assumed that they had fallen from the arch ceiling in generations past.

I was content to walk under that arch, and a few minutes later to make my way through tangled shrubs to the smaller arch as well, before returning to the vast room under the larger one. Holmes, however, was like a child, dashing back and forth, leaping like a goat from rock to rock, never betraying that he was in his late sixties. He found a narrow cave leading out of the base of the larger arch, disappeared into it, and soon reappeared in a completely different place, explaining that the passage had exited somewhere on the far side of the great rock. Then he was gone again, and when he returned a quarter of an hour later, he revealed that he had been to the top of the arch, climbing a ladder that had been built for that purpose by the locals who obviously used this place as an occasional picnic spot. Although I'm sure we could have spent longer there, we eventually returned to the truck and resumed our progress toward Rugby. We drove in silence for a while, until Holmes asked, "How close are we?"

"Not far now," said Willie.

"Then perhaps it is time to tell you why we have come here," Holmes replied. "I hope you don't mind having to listen to me reminisce, Willie.

"Not at all, Mr. Holmes," said Willie. "It is an honor, sir."

"Well, I don't know about that," he said. "In any case . . . As I said yesterday, I was asked to stop by here years ago by my brother, Mycroft. I was traveling from New Orleans to New York in 1893, and I assure you that before I had received information from my brother I had never heard of the Rugby colony.

"Mycroft had sent a package to me in New Orleans, delivered by a fast steamship of the British Navy. It contained several sets of instructions for upcoming tasks he wished for me to carry out. None of those are relevant to this tale. But included in the packet was the request to stop in Rugby, as a personal favor to Mycroft. He wished for me to deliver a message.

"The message was from the Earl of Nash and his older son, William Sexton, to their son and younger brother, respectively, Thomas Sexton, asking him to please come home to England. Thomas was one of those men who had come out to Rugby to participate in Hughes's dream of a perfect society. In addition to the message, Mycroft had sent the history of the whole unhappy family, which I read before I arrived.

"It seems that the family had estates in Somerset, near Frome. In years past the family's wealth had drained away, leaving them with a title and a great run-down house, but not much else. William and Thomas's father, the Earl, had made a new fortune in textiles, and with his increased wealth, had refurbished the family estates to their original condition. In the eighteen-eighties, the family lived there, with the Earl making regular trips to London and other cities to keep track of his interests.

"The family consisted of the Earl, whose name was Joseph Sexton, his wife, and his two sons, William, the eldest, and Thomas. There were no other children living. The sons were close in age, and had always spent much time together, although they were vastly different in temperament. William was somewhat studious, while Thomas was wilder, preferring to spend his time roaming outdoors. As they grew older, Thomas seemed to tease and bait his older brother, sometimes excessively, although William took it all good-naturedly.

"By the mid-eighties, both boys were in their early twenties, and William was obviously being groomed by his father to assume the duties of running the business, as well as someday becoming the next Earl. Although Mycroft made it clear that younger Thomas always knew that there would be a place for him in managing the textile mills, he seemed to resent it, as well as the fact that simply because he was younger, he was not able to inherit the title or much of the estate.

"As the young men grew older, Thomas's anger at his long-suffering and patient older brother continued to grow. On many occasions, Thomas picked fights with William, seemingly for no reason at all. During one of these, Thomas worked himself into such a rage that he grabbed a nearby pair of scissors and stabbed William in the arm. The family was shocked, but William kept insisting that it was an accident, and nothing further came of the matter.

"Throughout this time, William continued to be shaped for his future position, learning both the business and his responsibilities as a future earl. By the late eighties, William became engaged to be married to the younger daughter of a minor nobleman from Surrey.

"Unknown to anyone else at the time, including the young lady, Thomas himself had been interested for a while in William's new fiancée, although there was never any sort of real contact between the two. However, William's announced engagement was enough to inflame Thomas's jealousy even more. While William continued to prepare for his future, Thomas brooded about the house, sometimes disappearing for days at a time before returning smelling of drink. His parents, who loved him greatly, did not know what to do, and could not understand his growing rage at what he felt was an unfair arrangement. In particular, his mother seemed to suffer more and more as Thomas became increasingly wild and angry.

"These matters had continued for a number of years, until one night, not long after the engagement was announced, William became violently ill. His parents feared for his life for several days before he eventually recovered. As he rested weakly in his bed, the doctor spoke to the Earl and his wife, informing them that he believed that William had been poisoned. This was later confirmed through a privately hired chemist. The doctor did not know what circumstances might have led to this poisoning, but he felt that it must have been intentional due to the substance used, arsenic. However, he agreed not to call the police, and to let the Earl handle the matter.

"The Earl thought for several days, watching Thomas's behavior throughout that time. It soon became obvious to him that Thomas knew something about the poisoning. Finally he could avoid it no longer, and the Earl asked Thomas if he could

31

offer any information about the matter. To his surprise, Thomas readily confirmed that he had poisoned William, although he said it was not his intention to kill him. Rather, it was just to scare William, and that it had all been a brotherly joke. However, the longer Thomas talked, the more he worked himself into a rage, and the Earl was soon convinced that the poisoning had indeed been a murder attempt.

"When William was better, the Earl called in his wife and sons, and explained that he had given the matter a great deal of thought. It was with a heavy heart that he had decided that he had no choice but to send Thomas away. He could not have his own younger son arrested and prosecuted, but he also could not let the younger son try to kill the older.

"The family was shocked and dismayed, especially the boy's mother, who sobbed with grief. William himself argued to let Thomas stay. Thomas simply sat, stunned and feeling betrayed, in spite of the fact that he himself had tried to kill his own brother. When his father announced that he had arranged for Thomas to move to America, and to join the Rugby colony, Thomas simply stood, bowed, and left the room. He packed and moved out that night.

"It was several days, however, before Thomas was scheduled to depart. He seemed to be in perfect agreement with the plan, and was visited several times by both his father and William. The meetings seemed to be cordial, but strained. On the night before his departure, Thomas attended a dinner at the family home, where the participants were civil, if somewhat saddened and subdued by events. Thomas said goodbye to his father and weeping mother, and reluctantly shook hands with his brother before departing.

"The next morning, a pair of prostitutes presented themselves at the home of William's fiancée. They proceeded to relate a vile — and totally spurious — tale about their supposed long-standing relationship with William. One claimed to have married William the previous year in Penzance, while the other said she had proof that she had borne William a child. The women stated that unless they received one thousand pounds, they would relate their story to the press.

"Of course, no blackmail was paid. The fiancée's father contacted the Earl, who quickly showed that the rumor was an ugly lie. Further investigation, in the form of arresting the prostitutes and learning their story, revealed that they had been hired by Thomas several days before his departure, and coached specifically in whom to approach and what to say in order to ruin William's reputation.

"William was absolved of the lies, but it came out what his own brother had tried to do to him. William attempted to reconcile with his fiancée. However, the young woman was shocked and scandalized, nonetheless. Within days, the engagement was called off.

"At the same time the prostitutes were relating their fabricated story, Thomas was boarding a train to the coast, where he would catch a ship to America."

The trees had begun to thin as we listened to Holmes's story. The ground around us flattened into fields, many overgrown, but some with occasional early summer crops reaching toward the sunshine. I thought of the happy family with whom we had stayed the night before, and felt all the more the sadness of the Earl's family, and how it had been hurt by one young man's jealousy and anger.

"My brother, Mycroft, was a longtime friend of the Earl, and during this time he learned some of the Earl's difficulties," Holmes continued. "The next time the Earl was in London, Mycroft made a point of inviting him to dinner, where the whole story came out.

"Thomas arrived in America, and proceeded to Rugby as planned. I suppose one might expect that a person of Thomas's nature would have done something else instead, possibly falling into hard times, and certainly not followed through on his father's plan to join a rural agricultural colony. But Thomas appeared to be willing to give his new future a chance. The distance between himself and England, and his family, appeared to calm him. He arrived at Rugby, and was soon a hard-working and respected member of the community.

"Not much is known specifically of Thomas over the next few years. He seems to have fit in well with his peers, been active in the community events and opportunities, and generally managed to make a new home here. In the meantime, the Earl's family was devastated. William was heartbroken, both at the loss of his future wife, as well as by the treacherous actions of his brother. He was a good man, and could not understand why his brother, whom he unconditionally loved so much, hated him so, for no comprehensible reason. Thomas's mother seemed to age overnight, and she became ever-more weaker. Her health had never been good during the best of times, and Thomas's actions and subsequent departure had accelerated her declining condition. The Earl was in a similar plight, as worry for both his wife and William wore him down as well.

"In the meantime, Thomas built a home in Rugby, married, and had a child. His new wife was the daughter of one of the other colonists, who had brought his family here in the early days. Finally, Thomas seemed to have found a place to be happy. However, by this time, the early nineties, the colony itself was somewhat in decline, and Thomas's luck was about to change. In late ninety-two, his wife took a sudden fever and died. He was alone after only a year of marriage, and forced to raise his very young child by himself. The community attempted to step in and help, but the death of his wife seems to have reawakened the old Thomas. He became bitter and withdrew from the community. His house fell into disrepair, and as time went on, it became obvious that his child suffered from some sort of long-term, debilitating illness. Thomas began to feel cursed, and he would often tell whomever would listen that it was the fault of his family, back in England. His rants soon made him so unpopular that the rest of the residents began to avoid him whenever possible.

"The Earl had managed, with Mycroft's help, to keep track of Thomas in the colony, and he was initially cheered that Thomas was living a successful life. When he became aware of the death

34

of Thomas's wife, as well as the poor health of the grandchild that he had never seen, he resolved to do something to help his estranged son.

"He discussed the matter with Mycroft for some time, and it was finally decided to offer passage to Thomas and his child back to England, with the promise of forgiveness and a fresh start. Should Thomas not wish to leave his new life in America, the Earl was prepared to send him a small fortune in order to improve his circumstances. This was in the spring of 1893, and Mycroft explained to the Earl, in confidence of course, that I was not actually dead. In fact, I was working on something for Mycroft in the southeastern United States at that moment, and Mycroft would be happy to divert my path in the direction of Rugby if the Earl wished me to relay the message.

"The Earl graciously accepted the offer, and Mycroft then sent a message to me. He included a narrative of the family history with the packet he dispatched to me in New Orleans. And that is how I ended up in Rugby the first time.

"I do not recall exactly how I reached Rugby that day. It may have been by way of that town you mentioned yesterday, Willie. Rockwood, I believe you said. In any case, I did not approach from the direction we are traveling this morning. My route was much more genteel, arriving by rail in the small town, and then riding in a well-kept carriage down a tree-lined road, passing the occasional fine home.

"In those days, Rugby had somewhat passed its glory days, but it was still a showplace, with several hundred fine houses of varying architectural styles. I took a few minutes to walk around the streets, admiring this plucky British colony. I examined the library and its proud collection of over seven thousand volumes. I was quite amused to see several periodicals with your stories in them, Watson.

"Eventually I asked my way to Thomas Sexton's residence. Even without directions I fancy that I could have identified it. It was much more rundown than the neighboring houses, with weeds growing in the yard, pickets missing from the fence, and peeling paint and bare patches on the house boards.

"I had knocked several times with no response before I finally heard the sound of movement deep within the house. The door flew open to reveal a man who appeared to be in his forties, although I knew that he was only in his early thirties. A stale sour smell rolled out of the house, and behind the man I could see that all the curtains and blinds had been drawn, leaving this house in a depressing midday darkness.

"I introduced myself, and asked if I was speaking to Thomas Sexton.

" 'Yes,' he replied, 'and if it's about the bill for the medication, I'll tell you the same thing I told your employer. You'll get paid when I get the money, and if you do anything to withhold the medicines in the meantime, I'll see you are all held responsible for what happens!'

"I quickly explained that his assumption was mistaken, and that I was not there about payment for medication. Rather, I had been sent by his father, the Earl, to ask if he would not consider returning home. Failing that, I let him know that his father was prepared to offer him a substantial amount of money to ease his current conditions.

"He was silent for several moments, staring past me. Finally, he said softly, 'Does my brother still live?'

" 'Yes,' I replied. 'He has never married, and spends his time alternately between helping with your father's affairs and doing good works.'

" 'Then,' he said, taking a step back, 'You can tell them both to go to hell.' With that he shut the door. As I heard him turn to walk away, his muffled voice came through the door. 'And you, too!'

"I knocked several times more on the door, and walked around the house, pounding on the back door as well, but there was never any answer. I went back several times that same afternoon and evening, again with no response. I spoke to several people in town, and they confirmed that Thomas's condition was becoming somewhat strained, and that his baby son appeared to be suffering from some sort of wasting illness. I wrote a letter to Thomas, explaining again his father's offer and urging him to

36

accept it. I then took some of the money I had with me and spoke to the chemist, paying the outstanding debt for the child's medicines, as well as arranging the purchase of additional medication for several months into the future. I also let him know the address in England of Thomas's father, and told him that all debts would be taken care of if only the Earl were notified.

"There was nothing else that I could do. My schedule required that I return to New York as soon as possible, and I could not force Thomas Sexton to accept his father's charity. I continued on the next day, pursuing Mycroft's errands. At a later date, I was able to wire Mycroft my singular lack of success during the visit to Rugby.

"The next year, some months after my 'resurrection' and return to England, I happened to call on my brother at the Diogenes Club, only to find that he already had a visitor in the Stranger's Room, the only place in the entire club where conversation can occur. The visitor was William Sexton, who was now the Earl of Nash following the death of his father a month or so before. Mycroft introduced me to the Earl as the man who had visited his brother in 1893. William was a pale, gray fellow, quite thin in a stooped, scholarly way. When he learned who I was, his face lit up with sudden color, and he grasped my hand, asking for every detail I could remember about his brother, Thomas.

"It saddened me to have to relate the circumstances in which I had found his brother, as well as the reception that I had received when relaying the Earl's offer. I considered withholding part of the story, but I was uncertain how much had already been told to him by Mycroft, and so I told him everything. He did not seem surprised, and the initial joy at meeting me faded into the persistent chronic sadness that hovered about the man.

"Later, after William had departed, Mycroft told me that William and Thomas's parents had died not long after I had visited Thomas in Rugby. Mycroft had not doubted that the sadness resulting Thomas's final rejection of them had led indirectly to their deaths. Over the next several years, after that

37

meeting in the Stranger's Room, I heard of William, the current Earl, as he continued to perform the good charitable works that he had begun as a young man. He never married.

"I saw him again, one last time, not long after the end of the War. I was traveling near Frome, and my name appeared in the newspaper, against my express wishes, in connection with a trifling matter there. The next day, I received a small note at the inn where I was staying, from William. He stated that he had seen my name in the paper, and asked me to visit him."

By this time, we had arrived in Rugby. It had been over forty years since the optimistic little community had been founded. After the death of the founder in the mid-nineties, a slow malaise and decline had obviously settled on the area. Now, there were only a few dozen standing houses. There was no inn, and no one building that seemed to serve as a center of the community. Holmes paused in his story for a moment, and we all took a few moments to look around. None of the residents seemed to be outside, and we felt the illusion that we had the place to ourselves. Holmes looked into the distance, toward a church steeple rising above trees in the early afternoon haze. "Drive that way," he said.

We rode in silence for a few minutes, before Holmes resumed speaking. "At my last meeting with William, he informed me that he was dying. His life, he felt, had been a good one, but it had been full of regret at the pain caused by the separation from his brother, whom he loved but could not understand. He did not know why Thomas had hated him so, and he knew that now he never would know, at least not in this world. In spite of his brother's rejection, William had continued to keep track of Thomas since that day we spoke at the Diogenes Club in 1894. He told me some of what had happened since, and that Thomas had remained in Rugby. It was William's wish that I would pass on a message to his brother, should I ever find myself in this part of the world again.

"I let him know that it was highly unlikely I would ever be returning to Rugby. He said he understood that, but just in case, he wished me to promise him that I would relay the message.

38

'Promise me, Mr. Holmes,' he whispered, a man wasted by illness, lying alone in a large bed on bright, sunlit sheets. 'I don't know whom else that I could ask.' He fumbled on the bedside table and gave me an object, folding my fingers around it with his own. 'Take that to him. So he will know what you say is true.'

"I promised him. I told him that if it were ever possible I would relay the message, never believing that I would ever be back here to do so."

Willie pulled the truck to a stop beside the old church. Opening the door and dropping to the ground, Holmes said, "When I knew that we were coming to North Carolina, I brought the object with me, thinking we might have an opportunity to travel here as well."

Willie and I were standing on the ground beside him, as he turned to walk away. For one shocked instant, I thought I might understand. What if Thomas had redeemed himself, and found some worth in his life? What if he was the minister at this little church? What if he had made up for the pain he had caused for his family, doing good works in this small forgotten village?

I began to see that my hope was wrong when Holmes made no effort to enter the church. Instead, he walked along the side of the building, and I began to feel a little cold inside, in spite of the sunshine.

"William had kept track of Thomas," Holmes said, over his shoulder as we followed. "He sent money here, but there was never any acknowledgement. None of the local creditors ever sent any bills to London, as I had instructed them to do during my original visit."

We had reached the back of the church, and Holmes led us through a small iron gate into a fenced, poorly tended cemetery. The decline of the community was painfully obvious when observing the leaning, overgrown tombstones and shabbily painted church. Holmes began to move systematically among the graves, stepping respectfully over them when necessary, intently reading the carvings on the markers. Some took longer to decipher than others. Finally, on the far side near the rear fence, in a somewhat sunken area below a ragged pine tree, he stopped in front of three stones. "Here," he said softly.

Although I did not want to go over there, I joined him. Willie was silent at my side. We stood on either side of Holmes, staring down at the three lonely graves and their cheap stones. That area of the cemetery was in a low spot, and the rainwater runoff from the church and the rest of the cemetery had carved an eroded path across these graves. There was no grass here, simply exposed reddish earth, pebbled with countless bits of protruding gravel and mica.

The gravestone on the left was smaller and somewhat older, reading simply, "Jane Powell Sexton 1870-1892." In the center was a smaller stone, topped by a worn and moss-encrusted carving of a lamb. On it were the words "Joseph William Sexton, b.1892 d.1894 Beloved Son." To the right, a slightly larger stone read "Thomas Sexton, b.1863, d.1896 Far From Home."

Holmes fished in his pocket and produced a heavy gold ring, bearing some sort of family crest. He wiped it on his waistcoat, and turned it in the sun as he examined the results. Apparently satisfied that it was clean, he knelt down and pushed the ring into the loose soil of Thomas's ill-kept grave. Then he rose and stood silently for some minutes, his arms hanging and his hands folded together while he looked at the stone. Overhead, a mockingbird sang with uncontrolled joy in the June sunshine.

"Your brother sent you a message, Thomas," Holmes finally said, speaking softly but clearly. "He loves you. He always did." After another minute, he added, "And he forgives you."

Holmes turned and walked away. Willie soon followed, but it was several minutes before I joined them. We climbed in the truck and drove away.

The Adventure of the Madman's Ceremony
HOLMES AND WATSON IN TENNESSEE (PART II)

"We really are quite unaware of so much that happens around us," stated Mr. Sherlock Holmes, as we sat in a lurching truck moving through the surrounding forest. We had been discussing the unseen events that were occurring in the all-encompassing woods during every minute, as animals, insects, water creatures, and microscopic beasts struggled, lived and died in their own epic dramas that would never be known or recorded by man.

Although I understood that Holmes's statement referred to the conversation we were having then, his words could well have applied to the small town we would soon visit. There, the residents were completely unaware of the sinister events threatening to take place within days, or that evil itself was about to be revealed in their midst.

As I have related elsewhere, Holmes and I traveled to the United States in May and June of 1921*. While waiting for events to conclude during our initial investigation in Linville, North Carolina, Holmes and I spent nearly two weeks traveling in eastern Tennessee. It was during the first part of this visit that I was able to become acquainted with a distant relative, Rebecca Watson Marcum, and her family, living in one of the northern Tennessee border counties.

---

* EDITOR'S NOTE: See "Sherlock Holmes and the Brown Mountain Lights", edited by James McKay Morton (Mountain Living Magazine,1977-78), and www.carolina.cc/sherlock.html. See also "The Affair of the Brother's Request" in this volume.

41

After meeting with my distant American cousins, Holmes and I had been taken through the nearly untouched wilderness by Rebecca's son, Willie, to a wayside train station in the small town of Rockwood, Tennessee. Along the way, we had made a short stop in Rugby so that Holmes could fulfill an old promise.

Rugby was started in the eighteen-eighties as a social experiment, where younger sons of the British upper classes could come and work and live in an agrarian community while retaining the civilization and culture of their forebears in England. The effort was failing by the mid-eighteen-nineties, and at the time we passed through, only a few houses were left of the once-thriving colony.

The day was turning toward a pleasant afternoon as we passed through Harriman, having wandered through more of the same rugged and dramatic landscape that we had traversed that morning. Willie explained that Harriman had originally been founded as a temperance community. It was another attempt at a wilderness Utopia, much like Rugby, where we had been visiting just a few hours before. The original inhabitants of Harriman had soon failed in their purpose, but the town remained, apparently surviving due to its proximity to the coal trains that regularly passed through.

Willie indicated that it might interest us to visit in Harriman for a day, after having seen Rugby, but I could tell that Holmes was ready to return to Knoxville. Soon we reached the train station in nearby Rockwood.

We stopped on the main road by the station, seeing more cars than we had the previous day in Oneida, where we had arrived to meet Willie and his family. The town was laid out alongside the railroad tracks, which traversed from east to west at the base of a great mountain that loomed over the northern horizon. At the top were numerous rocky crags, hardly covered by the scrub trees that managed to root there. I was certain that the view from those heights would be wonderful, but at my age, I would never think of attempting the climb. Unless there was an unseen, easier way to the top, I doubt if many of the residents ever did.

We were in time to catch the last train of the day back to Knoxville. I tried to give Willie money in order to stay at some local lodgings for the night, as I felt that it was too late for him to return through the woods to his parents' home. He did agree that he would stay in town, but he refused to take any of the money both Holmes and I urged upon him. Finally, we said our goodbyes as the train seemed ready for imminent departure.

"A fine young man," said Holmes as we found our seats in the half-filled carriage. "You can be proud of your relations in the colonies, doctor." I agreed, and we did not speak again for several hours, as we each settled in for the long journey and prepared to read the newspapers purchased before boarding the train.

We reached Knoxville after dark, and again stayed at the small hotel near the river, as we had done several nights earlier. After finding something to eat, I returned to my room, while Holmes decided to explore the small city by night. After urging him to be careful, we separated. I went to bed early, somewhat sore from the past two days of riding in a truck over very uneven terrain.

A knock on my door the next morning revealed Holmes, as neat as ever, and apparently completely unscathed by his explorations of the previous evening. "Good morning, Watson," he cried. "Ready for breakfast?"

"An old military man never turns down the chance for a meal," I replied. "A soldier never knows when the next one might be."

"Oh, I venture to say that we shall safely remain in civilized territory for a day or so," he replied.

After breakfast, we strolled up the street for several blocks, and down a side street toward what sounded like a great deal of activity. Rounding a corner, we saw the city's market house, doing only moderate business on this mid-week morning. Various vendors were set up throughout the site, dealing in vegetables, poultry and meat, and other farm products.

"Not quite Covent Garden Market, is it?" I asked with a smile.

"Indeed," replied Holmes, before stepping away for a moment to speak with a heavy-set and jolly man selling honey. While he and Holmes had a short and esoteric discussion of joys and sorrows of keeping an apiary, I explored the adjacent stalls. I discovered a little old woman selling a confection called a fried pie. It appeared to be some sort of bread-like crust, folded over a mashed fruit filling. The edges were pressed closed, and the entire thing was fried in oil and then covered with a sprinkling of sugar. In spite of the fact that I had just eaten breakfast, I purchased one of the apple pies. While the woman watched, I devoured it in three bites. I smiled my pleasure, and she simply nodded.

"You have pie filling on your mouth," said Holmes, joining me.

Wiping my lips with my handkerchief, I urged him to try one of the pies, as well. He selected a peach pie, which I had not noticed. As he finished his pie and announced that it was delicious, I purchased another peach pie for myself.

"For later," I said. Then I noticed that Holmes had made a purchase as well.

"For comparative purposes?" I asked, nodding toward the small bottle of honey that he held.

"I am curious," he replied, "about the taste of honey gathered from American clover by American bees. As you know," he continued, as we walked out of the market, "the flavor of honey is affected by the flowers from which the bees gather nectar. You may also recall the matter several years ago when I discovered that Jonas Finley had been poisoned with honey made by bees that collected solely from poisonous plants."

As we walked, Holmes asked if I had any objections to remaining in the local area for a few days. "We are not due back in Linville for a while, and I have some research that I can do here, if it suits you."

"By all means," I answered. "I will visit the local college again, and perhaps see some of the other sites in and around the area."

For several days I did just that. Holmes spent his days at the University of Tennessee, located less than a mile west of Knoxville, while I looked at some of the downtown buildings. On one afternoon, I hired an automobile and traveled west out of town, along an excellently engineered rural road, admiring the well-tended farms and occasional larger houses. On the second afternoon I stopped at a fine old brick house, ten or eleven miles from town, with the intention of asking for some water. I ended up visiting for several hours with the gracious hosts, learning some of the more interesting details of Knoxville's history, as well as that of the house where I was visiting. It was reputedly haunted by the ghost of a man killed it he Civil War. I saw no signs of him, however, and when I mentioned it to Holmes that night, he simply scoffed.

On the morning of the fourteenth of June, a Tuesday as I recall, Holmes asked if I had any objections to moving our base of operations slightly south. "None at all," I replied, setting my coffee cup down on the breakfast table. "May I ask why?"

"Just a little more research," he replied. "I have spent the past several days examining some of the American newspapers for the last few years. The University library has an excellent selection, and my researches were as easily carried out here in this picturesque little town as they would have been elsewhere.

"Yesterday I received a message, forwarded from England, from an old acquaintance, Mrs. Mary Thaw, widow of the famed Pittsburgh railroad mogul and philanthropist."

"The wife of William Thaw?" I asked. "Wait," I said. "Surely she is not the mother of the infamous Harry K. Thaw?"

"One and the same," Holmes replied. "You know of the case?"

"I followed the news reports of the murder and subsequent trial with some interest. It was in 1906, I believe. You were living in Sussex by then. Isn't Thaw still in a hospital for the insane?"

"Yes, for at least the past five years."

"Don't tell me that you know Mrs. Thaw due to some sort of involvement in the murder of Stanford White?"

"Thankfully, I had no involvement in that seamy affair," Holmes said.

I recalled the details of the case quite clearly, in spite of the fact that they had taken place a number of years before. Mrs. Thaw's son, Harry K. Thaw, had grown up a troubled and sometimes violent young man. In his early thirties, he had become increasingly unstable, and he irrationally blamed more and more of his problems on a young architect, Stanford White. His paranoia increased, as did his anger toward White, although as I understood it at the time, White was probably innocent of any questionable actions toward Thaw. At some point in the early 1900's, Thaw fell in love with a chorus girl named Evelyn Nesbit, who had been romanced in the past by White.

Thaw began to pay frequent visits to the girl, spending a great deal of money on her, and taking her to Europe on several occasions. Over several years he begged her repeatedly to marry him, but she always refused. Eventually, however, he overcame her resistance and they were wed. In part, this occurred because Harry Thaw's mother begged Evelyn to marry her son, as she hoped it would be some sort of stabilizing influence on him.

Harry Thaw continued to show the same instability that he had displayed his whole life. After marriage, he appeared to lose interest in Evelyn, often traveling for long periods without her. Finally, in early 1906, Harry and Evelyn went together to Europe. On their return to New York, they happened to see Stanford White at a restaurant. This seemed to reawaken Harry's jealousy. Harry learned that White would be attending a show that evening, a performance that the Thaws were already planning to see. That night, Harry wore a heavy black overcoat to the theatre, and refused to take it off, in spite of the evening's heat.

He wandered erratically through the audience during the performance, approaching White several times before veering off. Eventually, at the end of the show, he approached White and shot him three times in the face. White was killed instantly.

The crowd had initially believed the entire incident to be a joke, or part of the show. Harry Thaw walked through the crowd with the gun held high above him, collected Evelyn, and departed. Soon Thaw was arrested. His first trial ended in a jury deadlock. Mrs. Thaw, Harry's mother, urged Evelyn to testify at the second trial that Stanford White had abused her, and that Harry had killed White in an effort to protect her. Evelyn was promised a great deal of money and a divorce from Harry if she so testified. Evelyn did so, and Harry was found not guilty by reason of insanity. He was placed in a mental hospital for the criminally insane, where he resided for several years before his release. In the meantime, Evelyn was granted her divorce.

I recalled that the events of the White murder had been heavily reported in the British press at the time. Seamy murders amongst the American rich were always of great interest to the masses, on both sides of the Atlantic. The later details of Thaw's life were less clear, but I thought I recalled one further fact.

"Wasn't Thaw arrested a year or so after his release for some other violent act?" I asked.

"Yes," replied Holmes, "He was convicted of assaulting and horsewhipping a teen-aged boy. He was again judged insane and returned to an asylum, as you mentioned, where he currently resides."

"Surely Mrs. Thaw does not want you to look into the matter of her son's current conviction?" I asked.

"Luckily, no," said Holmes, "and I would not do so if she did ask. I have no interest in becoming involved in the lifelong madness of Harry K. Thaw. People will be discussing him for years, and I do not wish to have my name associated with him.

"Mrs. Thaw has something much more sedate in mind for me. It seems that she has pledged a large amount of money to a local college near here, in order that they might construct a new building. However, some whispers of possible corruption at the institution have reached her ears in Pennsylvania, and after learning that I was nearby, she asked if I would discreetly look into the matter."

"How did she know that we were here?" I asked.

"It seems that we were observed by someone a few days ago when we were in Blowing Rock, at the Green Park Inn. This

47

person, a crony of Mrs. Thaw's, recognized us, and happened to mention that we were in North Carolina. Mrs. Thaw, using those speedy and efficient resources available to the very rich, verified the fact by cabling England. She determined that a message sent there could be forwarded to us here in America. She then sent a wire, which followed until it found us. I sent a return message, informing her that we were indeed in the United States, although we had now moved from North Carolina to Knoxville, Tennessee. She replied that it was very fortunate that we were here, as the college she wishes me to investigate is located only fifteen or twenty miles south of where we are seated now."

"How could a small college in this area have attracted the charity of a rich Pennsylvania family?" I asked.

"According to Mrs. Thaw," Holmes said, "one of the former presidents of the school approached Mr. Thaw in the 1860's. At that time, the school had been closed due to the Civil War, and the president was trying to raise funds to reopen it. Thaw sent a check for $1,000, which was used to buy the land where the current college is located. Thaw became very interested in helping the school, and gave a number of donations over the years, until his death in 1889. After that, his widow has continued to contribute, most recently giving a substantial amount of money to construct the large building on campus as a tribute to her late husband."

Pushing back from the table, I said, "That sounds like a pleasant way to spend a few days. Do you wish to leave this morning?"

Holmes was indeed ready to depart. Within a few minutes we had packed and checked out, and were on the local train headed south for the short journey.

"How did you initially come to know Mrs. Thaw," I asked, looking nervously down at the river as the train crossed over the narrow trestle bridge from the city side on the north bank to the rugged bluff on the south side.

"In 1913, when I was traveling in the United States under the name Altamont, I spent some time in various cities, cementing my reputation as an Irish radical. Starting in Chicago, I traveled

48

through numerous towns, including Pittsburgh, Pennsylvania. While there, I happened to come across a plot to sabotage some of the mining facilities and related railway connections. These happened to be owned by the Thaw family. I could not warn anyone as Altamont without taking the chance that my disguise would be penetrated. In the end, I slipped into the Thaw home, where I revealed my true identity to Mrs. Thaw. I can tell you that I had a few tense moments as that feisty woman held me at gunpoint while I urgently tried to explain why I was there.

"Once she understood what I was telling her, and more importantly, believed me, she wasted no time. She set her own forces in motion, quickly ending the plot, and all without ever revealing my own involvement. Over the years, we have corresponded sporadically, but she has never asked me to help her professionally until now. Thankfully, she did not seek to involve me in any of her son's defenses. I would have refused, and her goodwill toward me would have evaporated."

The train had picked up speed, and the cars settled down to a steady rocking as we left the points and junctions of the city behind us. The morning was beautiful, somewhat windy, but with skies as blue as I had ever seen them. It seemed no time at all that we were slowing. I expected to reach the station momentarily, but our fellow passengers showed no signs of preparing to disembark. I soon realized that the train had slowed to navigate a complicated series of parallel and intersecting tracks. In the distance I could see some of these running toward a large factory made of brick, belching smoke into the air from its tall stacks.

"What is that?" I wondered.

"I have no idea," replied Holmes. "I really do not know anything about this town we are visiting, although it has a pleasant enough name: Maryville."

The town, with its inclusion of my dear deceased wife Mary's name in it, saddened me for just a moment. Although Mary, my second wife, had been gone since 1893, I still missed her. My pain was increased by the recent passing of my third wife earlier in the current year. This entire trip to America had been partially due to Holmes's efforts to distract me in order to help me move past my mourning.

Eventually we traversed the crazed pattern of tracks and pulled into a small station. It was a fairly new building, set between two lines of rails, with platforms constructed all around the building to provide access to the trains on either side. On one side of the building were several warehouses, surrounded by horse-drawn wagons, automobiles, and trucks.

As our group disembarked, I noticed an equal number of people on the opposite platform, apparently waiting to depart on the return train to Knoxville. Everyone on our train had gotten off at the station, and I watched as it left, the empty carriages rocking as they were pulled away.

"This would seem to be the last stop on the line," I deduced. As Holmes nodded, a young energetic man stepped up to us.

"Right you are," he said. "The engine goes right up the line there to a turntable, where it will be reversed, re-attached to the cars, and returned to Knoxville." He stuck out his hand to me, shaking vigorously before moving on to Holmes. "Ray Rathbone," he said. "I'm pleased to meet you." He stepped back and looked at us. "You sound like you're from England," he said. We confirmed it, stating our names. He appeared to have no recognition of us, replying, "If you need anything here in town, I'm your man. I drive a taxicab," he said, jerking his thumb over his shoulder at one of the automobiles parked beside the station, "and I'd be happy to take you wherever you want to go."

We stepped to the side as a group of passengers moved past us to the stairs down from the platform. They walked together in a strange shuffling manner, their eyes all downcast. Holmes appeared to study them as they descended from the platform and walked away, and then he looked at Rathbone for a moment before stating, "We are going to be in town for a few days, while I do some research at Maryville College. Are we close? Can you recommend somewhere to stay near the college?"

Rathbone nodded. He was a stocky man, about twenty years of age. He was dressed in a worn white shirt and work pants, faded as well, but clean. His high hairline was damp in the morning heat, and he pulled out a handkerchief, running it across his brow, carefully avoiding the glasses with small, round, rimless lenses perched upon his nose.

"It's an easy walk from here to the college," he said. "Right up that hill, in fact. Usually it's only the students in the spring and fall, with their big trunks, that need any help getting there. As for a place to stay, well . . . " he said, and then faded into thought for a moment. "I know just the place," he exclaimed. Replacing the handkerchief in his pocket, he said, "I'll be happy to drive you there. It's about a mile past the college. I was just speaking to the woman who owns it this morning, and she said that she was thinking of renting out the little outbuilding behind her house. I'm sure she won't mind letting you use it for a few days. Right this way, gentlemen!"

We were led to an old Model T Ford, well on in years, but clean and excellently maintained. Rathbone stowed our few bags and held the doors as we entered. Within moments, we were bouncing across the tracks by the station and turning left onto the dirt street.

"You were right about this being the end of the rail line," Rathbone said. "We've only had an L&N spur from Knoxville to here for a few years. It's already changing things, though. The town is growing like crazy. Just two years ago, we got our first library, and an airplane even landed on a farm near here! We've started changing some of the street names to sound more like a city, and we even have a five-story building, which is more than you can say for most of the towns around here. Why, last year, our population grew to over thirty-seven hundred people."

As the vehicle bounced through several water-filled holes in the dirt street, Rathbone twisted the steering wheel from left to right, maneuvering his way out of town. "We just got a second fire truck," he said proudly. "In fact, Mayor Cox has even started talking about some sort of permanent road being built to Knoxville. I think it's a good idea, but a lot of people think it's a mistake. They say that ever since the railroad arrived here, we've started to grow too fast, and the whole nature of the area has changed."

On the left, fields stretched for a distance before revealing small residential neighborhoods in the distance. A group of buildings was prominent on our right as we motored past.

"There it is," said Rathbone, pointing to the buildings. Holmes, in the front seat, leaned his head, while I shifted in the rear seat to look out the right window. Almost immediately, we saw a tall white tower, topped with a flagpole flying the American flag. The tower was twenty or thirty feet tall, and rested centrally on a three-story red brick building. The bottom of the building was not visible, as our view was blocked by trees and bushes. On either side of the building were several wooden frame buildings, as well as a few brick structures of varying sizes. "That's Anderson Hall," said Rathbone. "That's the main building at the college. Those wooden buildings are dormitories for the students. There's a gymnasium, and a library, and some other buildings as well. In a minute you can see part of the college farm."

The road continued to climb slightly as we headed east, and in a moment we topped a low rise. In the distance, fifteen or twenty miles away, we could see the Smoky Mountains, as this part of the Appalachian range was named. The morning sun was over them, so they simply appeared to be one long, flowing, blue shape, where individual peaks seemed to blend together. In front of us, and quite a number of miles away, stood a mountain that looked to have three distinct and equal summits, sitting side by side. Rathbone noticed where I was looking and said, "Those are called 'The Three Sisters.' They're actually three separate mountains, well separated from each other, but the way they are lined up from this view, it appears that they are one mountain. And that," he said, gesturing to the right, "is the College Dairy Farm. The male students work there to earn money. Best milk and butter around."

"Male students?" Holmes said. "So the college is co-educational."

"That's right. The women work in the sewing shop. It just opened last year." He braked the car as we started down a shallowly-sloped hill.

"We're almost there now."

He negotiated a narrow one-lane bridge across a small stream that was joined on the south by a wide mere, filled with cattails and bobbing dragonflies. The bridge itself was about fifty feet in length. Holmes saw me notice it and smiled.

"It is rather like the bridge where Mrs. Gibson killed herself, is it not?"

"Indeed," I replied, recalling those events from so many years earlier.

Rathbone applied more power to the engine of his automobile, and we started up the slight hill on the other side of the stream. After another few hundred feet, we rounded a corner and saw a white two-story house, set back fifty feet or so from the road. Around it stretched several fields containing various crops, including young corn plants already standing a foot or so high. The fields extended behind the house for several hundred feet before joining a stand of trees that appeared to rise out of a lowland.

Parking the automobile in the drive, Rathbone opened our doors and led us onto the porch of the house. Before he could knock, the screened door was pushed open and a small woman stepped out with a welcoming smile. Rathbone introduced us, explaining that Holmes and I were from England, "to do some important research," he added mysteriously, and asked if the rooms that she had mentioned to him earlier in the day were available.

The woman, Mrs. Jones, stated that the rooms were available, and that they were located in the small building immediately behind her house and next to the barn. "If that's acceptable," she added. We readily agreed, and went with her to inspect the rooms.

I should add at this point that the woman's name was not actually Mrs. Jones. However, after the subsequent events that took place in Maryville, our temporary landlady recognized who we were, and she asked me to keep her name out of any future narrative that I might record of the matter. Honoring her wishes, I have changed her name to Jones. However, I must state that during the few days we stayed on her property, she was a most gracious hostess, and that we were fortunate to meet her.

About one hundred feet behind her house stood a large barn, with a small whitewashed cottage located to its right. The farm smell was strong here, both from the tilled soil of the nearby fields and from the livestock. However, it was pleasant and clean, and Holmes seemed happy that he was within walking distance of the college. Mrs. Jones pointed out that her fields and those of the college farm joined one another, and Holmes would be able to walk to the school either by the main road, or on the trails that crossed the properties.

Arrangements were made with Mrs. Jones regarding the short rental of the cottage. No meals were included, although she would supply us with linens. We settled our debt with Rathbone and retrieved our things from his cab. Holmes stopped Rathbone before he could climb back into his automobile. "Are you aware of any distant relatives you might have in England?" he asked.

"Possibly," Rathbone said. "How come?"

"Simply curiosity," Holmes replied. "Several days ago, Watson and I stayed with some of *his* distant relations, and this morning after hearing your name, I recalled that I am somewhat distantly related myself to the Rathbone family*. I did not know if you might have some information relating to your family history."

"As a matter of fact, I do," replied Rathbone. "Or at least, my sister does. I'll speak to her tonight, and let you know what I find out. You'll be here a few days, you say?"

"Yes," said Holmes. "I look forward to seeing you again."

As we unpacked our few belongings, I asked Holmes his

---

* EDITOR'S NOTE: See "The Case of the Very Best Butter" *The New Adventures of Sherlock Holmes* Radio Show (April 18, 1948) in which Holmes tells Watson that he is distantly related to the Rathbones.

plans. "I will go over to the college this afternoon, in the guise of a researcher. Actually, meeting Rathbone was fortuitous. I will use our possible family connection as a reason to examine local genealogy records, while also checking to see if anything appears to substantiate Mrs. Thaw's suspicions of possible corruption at the school. And what are your plans, Watson?"

I pointed to a small table beneath the rear window, facing a southern view across the fields filled with verdant growth. Some of the distant mountains could be seen over the tops of the trees rising from the lowland. "I will sit there for a while, catching up on my journals. Then perhaps a walk."

"Excellent," said Holmes. "Then we shall meet tonight for dinner."

And with that, he turned and left.

I stood for a moment before settling at the table. I spent a few minutes describing the events of the last few days within my journal. Soon, however, my memory returned to the small bridge we had recently crossed in order to reach this house. The bridge was very similar to the one where Mrs. Neil Gibson had died, back in early October 1900. The initial antagonism between Holmes and Gibson had dissolved following Holmes's brilliant solution of the case, and a warm friendship had developed between the two. Holmes and I admired the humanitarian impulses shown by Gibson after his marriage to his second wife. It had been several years since I had visited Gibson's estate, but as I sat at the small table, all the details of those days investigating the mystery of Thor Bridge came flooding back to me.

Recently I had published an account of "The Mazarin Stone" in *The Strand* magazine, and I resolved that the next manuscript to be submitted would be the account of Mrs. Gibson's death. I had no doubt that the public would be gratified to learn of the strange events on that peaceful country bridge.

I wrote for an hour or so, I suppose, before I recalled that Holmes and I had never eaten lunch. Wishing that Rathbone and his cab had not departed, I left and began to walk back toward town to begin my explorations with a midday meal.

55

We arrived in Maryville on a Tuesday. I spent the rest of the week leisurely exploring the town, while Holmes used his days at the college. On occasion he visited with several local civic leaders, bankers, and such, couching his relevant questions within innocent ones. Once he visited the new town library, but found it decidedly lacking in the materials he required. On Wednesday afternoon, I ended my day's rambles at the college library, a small, attractive brick building with a large stained-glass window.

Holmes was finishing up his research, and I spoke for a few minutes with the college minister, Reverend Stevenson. He pointed out a few of the campus buildings, including the site where initial construction had begun on Mrs. Thaw's donated building, which would be the largest on the college campus. Some of the walls were beginning to rise from the foundations, surrounded by scaffolding. As Holmes prepared to leave, Stevenson invited us to tea on Friday afternoon, at a small home that had been built in the woods adjacent to the college dairy farm.

Holmes and I walked by the half-completed building, making our way down the trail that passed through the college farm, going towards Mrs. Jones's house. I started to take the wrong trail before Holmes corrected me. "I have already explored this area," he said, pointing toward the direction I had initially chosen. "That trail goes to a spring house, not far from the house where we are taking tea on Friday." He gestured to the numerous saplings growing within the fields around us.

"The college farm has only been in existence for two or three years, and it is already something of a failure," he said. "There are less than two dozen young men enrolled here who are involved in agricultural studies. There is talk at the college that within a year or so, the program will be discontinued, and this entire area will probably be allowed to return to woodland."

My own explorations had been pleasant, but rather without purpose. I spent several hours the first day walking along the main street, placed along a ridge-top, circled on three sides by the wide stream that seemed to be the initial reason for the town's location. I strolled through the nearby residential neighborhoods, before moving on to the college grounds, where I examined more closely the large, partially finished building being funded by Mrs. Thaw. I walked around the site, and then spoke for a moment with the construction supervisor, asking him about some strange openings in the ground next to the building's proposed foundation.

"Oh, it's one of them sinkholes, doctor," he said. "It happens a lot around here. There's limestone rock under this whole part of the county, and wherever you find limestone you'll find sinkholes." He gestured toward the low areas of the college farm behind us. "Down there you'll find lots of rocks sticking out of the ground, and some springs as well. There are numerous springs all along the bottom of the ridge where Main Street is built. This whole area is probably riddled with caves."

During my time walking about the town, I had noticed a number of small groups of people walking together, all displaying the same downcast mien that I had observed from the group at the train station the day we arrived. Talking with Rathbone one afternoon, I asked him if he knew anything about these people.

"Not really, doc," he said. "They've been showing up for a week or so. They get off the train and head out of town. I heard they're camping somewhere north of here. I suppose if they get to be any trouble they'll be asked to leave, but so far they're laying low."

On Thursday night, Mrs. Jones invited us to eat with her and her sons, a quiet group of young men who listened politely to our conversation with their mother before solemnly turning their attention to the food.

Later that evening, as Holmes and I strolled through the empty main street, I asked him if he was having any luck at finding indications of corruption.

"None, Watson. I suspect that Mrs. Thaw has simply become suspicious for no reason. Perhaps it is a function of her age. She is quite elderly now, you know." We stopped by an old brick church building, looking at the streetlights from the nearby main thoroughfare as they reflected off the building's windows. The structure was very much like other churches I had seen in England, and could have been picked up from any number of small British villages and placed here. The wind sighed through the tall trees growing within the adjacent cemetery.

"All has not been wasted, however," Holmes continued. "Rathbone stopped by yesterday with some of his sister's family papers. The connection between his family and mine is there, although somewhat convoluted. He did not seem to be as impressed with his English ties, however, as with those to a German family, which he can trace back much further."

Friday evening was spent at the small house on the college farm, inhabited by Reverend Stevenson and his wife. It was a pleasant brick building, with a high sloping roof, and much larger inside than it had seemed from without. I had an enjoyable time, and even Holmes appeared to be relaxed and in a good mood. The following day, I accepted an invitation from Stevenson to take a drive around the area, in order to see some of the more distant sites that I had missed during my strolls in town. Holmes chose to continue his research.

Stevenson showed me the locations of some of the original forts, or stations as they were called, that had been built by the first settlers to the area. Originally, the Cherokee had used this area, and in fact the great north-south Indian Warpath, stretching all the way from the northeastern United States to the far south, had passed through Maryville.

"A number of Indian attacks occurred at these forts. None matched the massacre of the British soldiers, however, in the mid-1700's."

Stevenson went on to explain that twenty or so miles south was an abandoned fort, Fort Loudoun, constructed well before the American Revolution, and manned for several years by British troops. The Cherokee Indians had held it under siege for a number of months before allowing the inhabitants to depart in safety, as long as they promised to return to England.

The troops, along with their families, had departed from the fort and traveled several miles before the Indians broke the agreement and massacred the entire British contingent. I was surprised to learn of this event, as I had always been under the impression that the American settlers' problems with Indians had taken place in the northeast, or later out west. I had grown up reading the works of Cooper, and later the stories of cowboys and Indians. When I had visited my relatives northwest of here several days earlier, the only mention of Indians had been the implication that they were ancient inhabitants, long gone by the arrival of the settlers.

Later in the afternoon, we motored north in his automobile, with the intention of seeing some of the marble quarries that lay along the Tennessee River. These had supplied some of the stone for several of the national buildings in Washington, D.C.. Off to the right I could see the large factory that I had observed on the day we arrived in town.

"That's the Aluminum Company," Stevenson said, pronouncing *aluminium* in the American fashion. "That is the largest factory building in the world. They manufactured their first aluminum last year." He explained that after the invention several years earlier of a process to produce relatively cheap aluminum from bauxite ore, a factory site was sought that would provide access to the abundant electricity necessary for the procedure.

The area north of Maryville was chosen due to its proximity to railways for transportation of the finished product. A hydroelectric dam was built many miles away, and electric lines were run across the countryside to the factory building. My minister friend showed his disgust as he related the story. "The dam was built in the mountains, making a mountain river into a lake, and using the water to power the electric generators. The community around the dam is known as Calderwood.

"When the Aluminum Company approached the state legislature for permission to incorporate a town, they provided a series of map coordinates where this town would be located. Everyone assumed that they would be incorporating the area around Calderwood. The new town was to be called 'Alcoa,' which stands for 'Aluminum Company of America.'

59

"What no one realized was that the map coordinates were not for Calderwood, the mountain town near the dam, but instead for a sizeable chunk of what we called 'North Maryville,' right over there around that factory," said Stevenson. "No one thought to actually look at a map to see where the new town would be, and the legislature approved it. Suddenly, the town of Maryville lost a third of its area, and had another town growing out of the top of it. This was all done, of course, so that any tax revenue generated by the place would go to the new company-owned town, and not to Maryville.

"I must admit," my new friend continued, "they are trying to make the place nice, for a company town. They've laid down streets, and built a number of houses, although many of them are completely identical to one another. There is talk of building parks there, as well. I suppose it will turn out all right. It's not as if anything would have been built there otherwise. The place was unofficially known as the 'Maryville Swamp.' Lots of groundwater there, poorly drained. I've even heard rumors of a cave or two."

The following Monday, Holmes continued his researches while I decided to visit Alcoa, and look more closely at the largest factory in the world. Little did I realize how the day would end. I walked into town, where I contracted with Rathbone to drive me to the factory in his cab.

He dropped me off and offered to wait, but I declined, wanting to explore for a while. I visited the main office of the great factory, and was given some slight information regarding the history of the aluminum separation process invented by Charles Hall, the company itself, and the decision to build a town here. However, I was soon given to understand that idle tourists were not encouraged, and I departed, intending to walk some among the nearby residential streets before returning to Mrs. Jones's farm.

As my new friend the minister had told me, many of the houses were identical to one another. They were all of wood frame construction, most only one story high. The entire area was clouded with the smoke from a hundred cook stoves and fireplaces. I noticed that several of the street names, Dalton, Maury, and so on, were named for famous scientists, while the significance of others, such as Vose, completely escaped me.

While strolling down Maury Street, I observed a young man standing in front of one of the rarer two-story houses, watering a young tree. All along both sides of the street, oak trees had been set out in rows several feet back from the roadway. In later years, I was certain that the tree-lined avenue would be quite beautiful as one traversed it. Now, however, the trees were little more than saplings.

The young man, probably in his early teens, spoke to me as I passed. I stopped and answered, complimenting him on the neighborhood and his house, which was well-kept. He informed me that his father was one of the company managers, and as such, was entitled to one of the larger two-story houses. At that moment a woman, obviously his mother, stepped out onto the porch. I introduced myself, and explained that I was exploring the neighborhood. "My name is Mrs. Wade," she said, "and this is my son, James." She graciously invited me in for some lemonade.

While Mrs. Wade stepped through the swinging door to the left of the fireplace, into the kitchen, I looked at the pleasant room. Stretching along the left side of the house, it had tall windows at the sides and rear. While somewhat dim this morning, I was sure it would be bright and cheerful in the afternoon. The house itself, a great square box, seemed to have only three rooms on the ground floor. The long formal parlor in which I sat took up the left half of the ground floor, while the other half contained the kitchen at the rear and a small dining room at the front of the house. The stairs must have been located somewhere behind the fireplace, between the kitchen and dining room.

The woman returned with the lemonade, and as we sat and talked, she asked polite questions about England. At some point during the conversation, I became aware that her son was becoming somewhat agitated. Finally, his mother could not ignore it any longer, and asked, "What *is* the matter, James."

He started to whisper, but she asked him to repeat it aloud. "He's Dr. Watson!" said the boy.

"Yes, that is his name."

"No, *the* Dr. Watson. Like in Sherlock Holmes!"

She looked at me anew, and raised an eyebrow, as if asking me to confirm or deny her son's statement. I acknowledged that I was that Dr. Watson, and stated that Holmes and I were visiting in town for a few days, but that we did not want knowledge of our stay to become widespread.

She thought for a moment, nodding to herself, and then stated, "Perhaps, since you are here, you and Mr. Holmes can offer an opinion on something that has been bothering me."

She proceeded to relate a tale so strange that I agreed to seek Holmes's help. She let me use her telephone. I managed to be connected to Maryville College, where I found someone willing to relay a message to Holmes, if he was still in the college library. In a while, Mrs. Wade's telephone rang. It was Holmes, to whom I repeated the basics of her story. Within twenty minutes, he was stepping to the curb in front of her house from Rathbone's cab. He indicated that Rathbone should wait.

Young James appeared to be stunned as he watched Holmes energetically walk up the front walk to the house. Mrs. Wade gave no such impression, ushering Holmes in and offering him lemonade and refreshments. When he had his glass in hand, I had her repeat for him what she had told me.

Essentially, her story concerned recent goings-on in a nearby clearing. "It has become something of a neighborhood park," she said, explaining that the aluminum company, which owned all the houses and property in the town, intended to improve the location eventually, "building recreational areas, and schools." In the meantime, however, the vast fields had remained a wide open space, cleared and mowed, but with numerous old-growth trees allowed to remain, shading the various havens created by the meandering brook that wandered through the tract.

"The small stream is formed from several springs that rise near a hillside in the center of the parkland. The hill is more of a small cliff, really. The largest of the springs, a rather wide sandy pool, is near this small cliff, which is something of a rocky outcropping exposed in the hillside.

"At the base of these rocks is a wide crack in the earth, extending back at a downward angle, out of sight and into the darkness. The crack extends thirty feet or more from left to right, and is only one or two feet in height at the entrance. A cold breeze blows from it, and animals shy away from the place. In fact, during the times I have walked there, I do not recall birds even sitting in the nearby trees to sing.

"As James can tell you, I often take strolls in the mornings, and I frequently go by the place of the springs and the cliff, to look at the wildflowers growing among the rocks. In spite of its eeriness, I have never felt any fear or nervousness about the place. I believe that a cavern of some sort begins there, and that would probably explain the excessive number of springs around this area. I have read something of geology, and I understand that areas such as this, with a large number of rocky outcroppings sticking up out of the ground, are indicators of high groundwater, as well as caves and sinkholes."

Holmes nodded. "It is known as a *karst* area."

"Exactly," said Mrs. Wade, nodding. "In any case, we have lived here for a couple of years now, and nothing has changed until just recently. In the last week or so, a great number of people have been arriving in town and making their way to that park, setting up campsites throughout the fields. They are quiet enough, I suppose, but they do not belong here. They have even taken to walking through our neighborhood, sometimes knocking on doors and asking if they can buy eggs or bread. I thought that Dr. Watson was one of them when I saw him talking to James earlier. I rushed out to send him away, and I was so relieved to learn that the doctor was not one of the strangers that I invited him in for lemonade.

"Several of the residents have complained to the company, which owns the land, but we were put off by Mr. Timmons, one of the managers who seems to have given them permission to camp there. He stated that they are part of a religious group, here to celebrate one of their holy days, and that once they are done

63

they will go. Mr. Timmons's wife is said to be a member of that faith, and possibly Mr. Timmons is as well. It was because of this relationship that the strangers knew to come here in the first place, and why he gave them permission to stay here."

Holmes and I looked at one another. We had both seen some of the people to whom she referred over the last few days, as the groups were arriving in town. We had discussed them on several occasions, and one evening as we smoked our pipes I had told Holmes what Rathbone had said about the group camping somewhere north of town.

"I went walking there this morning, as I usually do," continued Mrs. Wade, "making my way around the edge of their camp. The people were somewhat standoffish, but friendly enough, and I spoke to one of the group's women. She said that the festival they are celebrating will culminate tomorrow morning at sunrise. She implied there is something special about this particular gathering, and that they do not assemble this way every year.

"As I was leaving, I saw some of her laundry, a pile of folded white robes. A closer look showed that the robes were hooded, and embroidered on the shoulder was this emblem."

She leaned forward and picked up a piece of paper, turned face down until now on a side table. "I tried to draw it when I returned home." She held it up, showing Holmes the sketch of a symbol that I had instantly recognized when viewing it a few minutes earlier. Seeing it had been enough to make me reach Holmes immediately.

Holmes's eyes widened minutely, but he made no other movement or comment. Mrs. Wade leaned forward and handed him the paper, which he brought closer to his eyes. I knew what he was seeing.

Drawn on the paper was an egg-shaped circle, surrounded by the squeezing coils of a snake. The wide part of the egg was at the top, and hovering over it was the serpent's head. His tail jutted from the smaller end at the bottom. Shaded onto the oval behind the body of the snake were a pair of large dark spots, giving the impression of eye sockets, and making the egg into the death-head of a human skull. Around the outside edge of the oval were a series of small faint crosses.

Pointing to them, Holmes asked, "What do these small x's represent?"

"The stitching on the white robes was in much greater detail than I was able to draw," said Mrs. Wade. "I am not much of an artist, I'm afraid. There were actual diamond-like patterns on the snake's body, and its face wore an expression of crafty evil, almost gleeful and proud. Around the edge of the skull were a series of smaller symbols, rather like letters, but nothing like the alphabet that I know."

Holmes pulled a pencil from his pocket and wrote for a moment at the bottom of the page. "Did these markings resemble the embroidered writing you saw?" he asked, holding up what he had produced.

Mrs. Wade leaned closer and examined the sheet. "That looks quite similar to what I saw. Of course, I cannot say for sure."

Holmes nodded. "I am fairly certain that what I have written is correct, combined as it is with the skull and serpent design which you copied. I have made a small study of these symbols in connection with a past case. The writing is Ogham, an ancient Celtic script sometimes used by the Druids."

I had also learned something of the symbols on Mrs. Wade's paper years before, during an investigation in which Holmes and I were called to Stonehenge in order to determine who had chalked the serpent drawing on various menhirs in the ancient ruins. At the time, Holmes had taught me that the representation of a snake coiled around an egg was one of the ancient symbols of the creation of the universe, used variously by Egyptians, Indians, Druids, and even Freemasons. However, sometimes the symbol was polluted, changing the egg to a skull. I had no doubt that the text written by Holmes said exactly what had been written years before on the great monoliths at Stonehenge. Loosely translated, "For new life, first death."

Holmes looked at it for another moment. We both knew that the symbol, combined with the writing, was the ceremonial badge of death. I saw that he wished to pull out his pipe and smoke, but he would not ask to do so here in the Wade's home. Finally he looked up at me.

"Tomorrow is June twenty-first," he said.

I nodded. "At sunrise?" I asked.

"Most likely." Turning to Mrs. Wade, he asked, "Do you know of anyone that has gone missing in the last day or so? Any children? Any animals or pets?"

Mrs. Wade said, slowly, "No, no, I'm not aware of anything like that."

James interrupted, "What about Tyler?"

"Oh, well, there is Tyler," Mrs. Wade replied, with a small laugh. "Tyler Roberts. He's a young boy, several years younger than James. He lives a few doors up the street. He often disappears overnight. He likes to camp and hike. He's a very self-sufficient boy, and his mother has learned to stop worrying when he is gone. He wanders off all the time. I was not aware that he was away right now, but it is not unusual."

"He is gone," James said. "His mother asked me this morning if I had seen him. Usually he only stays away overnight, but he has been gone for two nights now. I think she is starting to get a little worried. And also, Mrs. Floyd up the street said that their dog is missing. Maybe it just ran away, but Mr. Holmes did ask about any missing pets."

"How old is Tyler," asked Holmes. "Please describe him."

"He is about twelve," said Mrs. Wade. "Small for his age, but very strong and scrappy. His skin is quite tanned and dark, but his hair is blonde, almost white. His skin is often covered in one place or another with scrapes and scratches from whatever outdoor mischief he has gotten himself into."

Holmes checked his watch, and then stood. "Mrs. Wade, I believe that what you have described in the nearby park is a gathering of individuals who are up to no good. I regret that I have to ask this, but I would like you to keep secret the fact that Dr. Watson and I have visited you this morning, and also what you have told us. Please do not discuss with anyone what you have seen in the park. I'm afraid that I must ask you and your son not to tell even your husband."

"That would be fine," said Mrs. Wade. "When I tried to talk to him about it before, he gave me to understand that I was simply being a busybody, and that in any case the people would soon be gone."

"Thank you," said Holmes. "Dr. Watson and I are going to discuss this matter with the local police. I think it is quite serious. I would like your permission to take James with us. In case we have any further questions, he will be at hand to answer them. He may be with us until tomorrow, if that is all right."

James immediately showed his eager agreement, and Mrs. Wade had no objection, although she did seem somewhat worried, and repeatedly made James promise to stay out of the way and to stay out of trouble. Thanking her again, and reminding her not to mention our visit, we departed in Rathbone's waiting cab.

When we directed Rathbone to take us to the police, he explained that the new city of Alcoa only had the beginnings of a police department, and that the city of Maryville had just appointed a police chief for the first time that year. "N.L. Brewer," he said. "Seems like a good man. Before we had a police chief, we made do with a town marshal."

At the courthouse in the center of town, we introduced ourselves to the chief, a seasoned man who carried himself with a military bearing, no doubt earned in the recent European war. Brewer listened with patience as Holmes explained his suspicions about the group camping near the Aluminum Company neighborhood. Holmes drew the symbol that Mrs. Wade had seen on the hooded white robes. James nervously told of the missing boy and dog. Finally, Holmes outlined what he believed was about to happen, and the significance of tomorrow's date.

Brewer listened with intelligent gravity, understanding exactly what Holmes was telling him. He did not seem to question either Holmes or the story, replying, "You were right to come to me, Mr. Holmes. I have also been noticing these people arriving in town for a week or so, and wondered what they were about. If someone at the Aluminum Company invited them, it is probably better not to involve the company. I have some men that I trust completely. We can use them. When do you want to begin?"

Holmes indicated that immediately would suit him. The chief set about finding his men, while Holmes and I explained the situation to Rathbone, whom Holmes had instructed to wait. Rathbone was eager to join us, and showed no surprise that Holmes and I had turned out to be more than simple visitors doing research.

By late afternoon, Brewer's men had gathered. They were carefully briefed on what to expect. A number of them were veterans of the War, and they all appeared to be exactly the type of men we would require that night. Weapons were issued to some of the men, while others made do with clubs fashioned from new axe handles purchased at a nearby hardware store. Now we simply had to wait until sundown.

Holmes had explained that the group we would be facing no doubt intended to have an initial bonfire ceremony after the sun had gone down. The revels would certainly last for hours, and to a casual observer it would seem curious but harmless. The ritual would likely turn sinister with the approach of sunrise on the next morning. The plan was to sneak into the Druids' camp after dark, when they were gathered at the bonfire. Holmes explained that we would still need to be quite cautious, as guards would likely be placed around the gathering. "Remember," Holmes said, "most Druids are harmless. It is the inclusion of this death symbol that makes these people more dangerous. All of them may be involved, or it may just be a few of the leaders. In any case, stay alert."

As the sun finally dimmed over the western horizon, we departed in a collection of automobiles, driving in a roundabout way to the far side of the parkland, so that we would not be observed by anyone in the houses that surrounded the park or the factory. Holmes, James, and I rode in Rathbone's cab. James had been allowed to accompany us, on the condition that he stay in the cab while we carried out our invasion.

Holmes had privately told me earlier that he wished to keep James close so the boy would not return home and be tempted to reveal our plans to his mother and father.

It was full dark when we and the other vehicles arrived. We were nearly half a mile north of the park, in an abandoned pasture on the far side from the company houses. The men around us formed up. With Holmes and the chief in the lead, we set out across the choked fields.

Our progress was slow due to the necessity of finding a path through brush and brambles in the dark, as well as the need to cross the occasional small brook or rill, produced by some nearby spring. If there was any moon, it was hiding behind the clouds. Several times I tripped over some of the karst stone showing above the plants. However, it was all small and insignificant compared with the great rocky tors that I had seen on Dartmoor many years before.

As we progressed, I began to be aware of the light of a great bonfire in the distance. It flickered and waved, and in front of it were countless black shapes, dancing and swaying as they rotated around it in some trancelike orbit. The wind was light, and blowing from the direction of the fire. I could sometimes smell smoke, and once or twice heard the eerie songs of the revelers as their monotonic chants were carried by the breeze.

The chief had known exactly which spot we meant when describing the great horizontal crack below the rocky cliff. It was only a hundred feet or so from where the bonfire was located. The fire burned on the top of a nearby cone-shaped hillside, its very brightness helping to make the surrounding areas seem much darker. Even though we were in shadows, the light from the fire reflected on the rock face of the stones above the cavern entrance. Suspecting that there might be guards, Holmes and the chief had arranged for two of the more stealthy men accompanying us, both big silent fellows, to move ahead and clear the way.

Our group paused in deep shadows as the two men, both stepping soundlessly, crept toward the open space before the rock. In a moment I heard the peculiar ringing sound of an axe handle striking another object, followed by a soft dusty thud as something sank to the ground. In a few seconds, one of the men returned, gesturing us forward.

The other man was tying a robed figure, lying unconscious on the ground. I knelt and examined him briefly. He would be out for quite a while, but his breathing was sound, and he would recover. In the meantime, Holmes was directing the men toward the crack. Only inside would they be allowed to use their electric torches. Initially, they must all crawl into the black passage in blind darkness.

I myself felt some trepidation, but none of the men showed anything of the sort. The chief went first, followed by Holmes. Then it was my turn, aided by a dark figure whose face I could not see. Only when he said, "Easy, doc," did I recognize that it was Rathbone, now dressed in dark clothing like the rest of us. It was the first time I had not seen him in his white shirt and light faded pants.

The crack dropped into the earth at a fairly steep angle. The floor entrance was dirt, pebbled with gravel, and the feeble light from the bonfire only revealed the first few feet. As I slid in feet first, I initially moved on my back. As the overhead rock loomed closer, I tried to turn so that I would be sliding on my stomach. I discovered that the awkwardness of turning while dropping only made me slide faster, and I experienced a second of blind panic as I pictured myself dropping ever faster before sliding off the edge of the entrance, shooting over a final lip of rock and falling into eternal darkness.

Almost immediately, however, hands grabbed me and helped me stand upright on the floor of the inner cave. I was pulled back as other men slid down into the spot where I had just stood. As my eyes adjusted, I could see that we were in a small chamber, approximately fifteen feet square, with the floor about four feet lower than the sloped entrance rock above me. The floor itself was stone, and dropped gradually toward the rear of the room, where an opening in the rock seemed to lead deeper into the earth.

The last men to enter brought the bound guard with them. He could not be left outside where his discovery would signal our presence. Holmes stepped over to the rear passage out of the room and snapped on his torch, shielding it with his hand. A path led down into the darkness. I joined him, followed by Chief Brewer and Rathbone. In the distance we could hear the sound of rushing water. With the others following, we moved deeper into the cave.

The passage only lasted a hundred feet or so before opening into a much wider room. While traversing the connecting corridor, I observed the walls and floor, which appeared to have been widened and formed at some point by tools. However, the marks and grooves on the walls and floor appeared to be ancient, and I idly wondered how long this site had been in use by men before tonight.

The large room we entered was about fifty feet across, and nearly twenty feet high. The ceiling was rounded, and there did not appear to be any stalactites or stalagmites whatsoever, as if they had been cleared out at some point to preserve the openness of the chamber. Numerous large boulders stood around the perimeter of the room, where the roof sloped down sharply to join the floor. Along the far side of the chamber, running from left to right, was an underground stream, only three or four feet across, its depth unknown in the near darkness. The surface of the water was a black mirror in the torch light, and it could have been six inches or six feet deep. I could see from the sides of the room that in times of great rains the water level would rise and fill the entire volume of the place.

Holmes walked around the room, examining foot scuffs in the mud on the floor. He gestured me to his side, and indicated a curious stone located centrally in front of the stream. It was carved out of the very floor of the room, left in place by the ancients, rising in one solid piece out of the ground. It was about six feet long and three feet high. Flat on top, it resembled a narrow table. Placed in the center of it, apparently there for future use, was a dagger. It was not beautiful craftsmanship. Rather, it had a homemade look, as if the metal had been shaped

71

and sharpened by pounding it with a stone. It looked very old, and in that setting, very evil. Holmes and I looked at one another. Our interpretation of the embroidered symbol had been correct.

Holmes called our group together and explained that we were not certain when the people at the bonfire would shift their location to this cavern. Therefore, the men would need to hide behind the rocks around the walls and wait, hidden, possibly for many long and miserable hours.

They were all hardened men, and they did not need to have any explanation about what was to come. Silently, each man took a position, two slinging the bound and gagged guard between them, and we all settled into our places of concealment. Holmes was the last, remaining in the center of the room with his torch until we were all in place. The other torches went out, leaving Holmes holding the single source of light. Then, he found a place near me, sank to the ground, and turned off the torch, plunging the cavern into darkness.

How to describe those hellish hours of waiting? The cool damp air of the room quickly permeated our clothing. The constant sound of the tumbling water in the stream, moving from God knows where to God knows where, soon became a maddening drone in my ears. Within minutes or hours, I could not tell, I was hearing what I thought to be voices murmuring in the dark. I knew that it was my imagination, but at times I was tempted to stand and remind everyone to be quiet, so certain did I almost become that people were carrying on conversations.

The worst, of course, was the darkness itself. It was absolute, and my eyes would not adjust. Countless instances I held my hand in front of my face, but I could see nothing. I am not a fanciful man, but there were times when I had to remind myself that I was sitting behind a solid rock on a solid floor, and that the darkness was not closing in on me. On another occasion, I became obsessed with the idea that the clouds I had observed earlier had thickened, and it had started raining outside. We would never know it, in this room under the earth, until the underground stream began to rise. Soon we would drown, trapped in the rock chamber, unable to ever find the exit before it was too late.

The only awareness I had of anything other than myself was the occasional movement beside me of Holmes as he shifted to a more comfortable position. I was certain that his disciplined mind was not misbehaving like mine, and that his hand knew exactly where the electric torch was, ready to turn it on at a moment's notice.

My watch would later reveal that it was somewhere after four in the morning, a half hour or so before sunrise, when we first became aware that someone was entering the cave. At first, I heard chanting, weaving its way into the eternal song of the underground stream. I believed that it was my imagination, but gradually the terrible music became louder, and I knew that it was real. Then my eyes, in the dark for hours, began to perceive the glow of light as it increased from the direction of the opening. The walls around it seemed blacker as the rude stone doorway grew brighter, illuminated by the first robed people entering the room, carrying smoking torches.

I shifted on the ground, keeping behind the rocks as I carefully observed the newcomers. They continued to enter, their feet scuffing through the dried mud, filling the center of the room, swaying and singing. Only a few held burning wood torches, so the light never became very bright. As the majority of the group finished entering the place, they started to shuffle, splitting into two groups and leaving a pathway between them leading from the entrance to the stone table on the far side by the stream.

A group of three men appeared in the door, taking solemn steps as if they were university dons participating in a convocation ceremony. The first man was tall and thin, and his white robes were decorated with numerous embroidered designs, leaf-like patterns winding about his shoulders and arms. He was obviously the leader, and a shudder passed through the crowd with his appearance. The droning of their chant never faltered.

Following him were two men, each in plain robes like those worn by the general followers. They were large men with stern expressions, and they each had their hands on the shoulders of two boys being pushed in front of them. From where I hid, I could tell that the boys' hands were bound behind their backs, and their mouths were covered with gags. The first was a small boy with very light hair. He was struggling as he was pushed forward with each step. The second prisoner did not fight his captor, and looked both right and left with terror in his eyes. He was James Wade, who was supposed to have waited for us with the automobiles.

As the boys were stopped in front of the raised platform, the chanting changed from a monotonous drone to some sort of words, in a tongue that I could not understand. It was full of sibilant hisses and odd tonal changes. In that setting it seemed extremely evil, as malignant as something uttered by the tempting serpent in the Garden. The pitch seemed to rise as the first boy, obviously the missing Tyler Roberts, was lifted onto the table and placed on his back, held down as he kicked and fought.

James watched from the side, terrified and still. I glanced at my watch in the dim flickering light. Outside, the sun would be rising on the morning of June twenty-first, the solstice, the first day of summer, the day of rebirth. The leader, from his place behind the sacrificial table, raised the ancient dagger and began to shriek in the vile language of the chanters.

"Stop!" shouted Holmes, standing beside me. The mass of robed figures paused, fell silent, and stared at him, but the leader continued his sing-song call as Tyler renewed his bound struggles. As the knife began to descend, I heard an explosive report beside me. The leader's hand snapped back, and the dagger flew away from him into the rushing stream.

At my side, Rathbone stepped around the boulder behind which he had hidden, a smoking pistol thrust in front of him. All around the room, other men were appearing, holding guns, rifles, and axe handles. One robed man bolted toward the cavern entrance, only to be stopped as an axe handle met his skull, dropping him instantly to the muddy floor.

The leader stood motionless, holding his bleeding hand above Tyler, who was staring up in fascination. The hand was now nothing more than a thumb jutting out from a ragged mess that was the remaining bottom half of the man's palm. Blood ran down his wrist, staining the sleeve of the white robe. Rathbone later explained that he had chosen to use expanding bullets in his revolver, which had caused the extreme damage to the leader's hand. Rathbone did not appear to regret his decision.

The boys were quickly freed, while I tended to the leader's shattered hand. As I bound it with strips torn from his decorated robe, I examined the man's face. He was expressionless, and appeared to be in shock. He gave no indication that the pain affected him at all. When he had entered the cavern he had seemed to be one of the most sinister and fearful figures I had ever seen. Now, up close and defeated, he was simply a middle-aged man, his face covered with the broken veins of the chronic alcoholic, and his shoulders and thinning hair flaked with dandruff.

It would later be revealed that his name was Lloyd Duff, and that he had founded this branch of Druid revivalists in England several years before. When that country became too hot for him, he had relocated to America, where he had continued his nefarious activities. Initially, he had been nothing more than a con man, playing on the weakness of those who sought false comfort in the rituals of ancient religions that they did not understand. Gradually, Duff began to believe in the hokum that he was peddling. He had sought out the darker side of the religion.

It was then that he became acquainted with the two men who had been herding the boys, Luther Simmons and Matthew Boyd. They were criminals from their early years, also originally from England, and they had exploited Duff for their own gain. Using Duff's corrupted knowledge of ancient Druid practices, they fashioned a new cult, which progressed from simply bilking the money of the worshipers to the occasional sacrifice.

It was discovered that Duff, Simmons, and Boyd were linked to several murders in England, related to their activities there before they fled to America. Eventually, they were extradited back to England, where Duff was tried and placed in a hospital for the insane, while Simmons and Boyd finally received their long overdue punishments in the form of poorly attended and barely reported executions.

The robed revelers, now with broken spirits, were herded from the room to the open ground outside. They huddled like sheep by the spring near the rock face. Vehicles were summoned to transport them in groups back to the county jail. As the sun continued to rise, Holmes and I verified that both boys were all right before they were sent home. A quick check revealed that Mrs. Floyd's dog, as well as several other pets, were all right, and were tied up in the Druid camps.

Holmes walked over to the man who had been knocked unconscious while attempting to flee the underground chamber. He was now awake and being questioned by Chief Brewer, who explained to us that the fellow was Mr. Timmons, the Aluminum Company official who had allowed the group to camp in the park.

"He says that he and his wife are long-time Druids, and that today is one of their holy days," said the chief. "He first discovered the cave a few years ago when he first moved to this area, and he could tell that it had been used in the past for ancient ceremonies. When Duff communicated with him about plans to pass through this area, Timmons suggested using the cave. Duff then finalized plans for his followers and recruits to meet here for this special day. Only after they had arrived did Timmons realize that Duff and some of the others were not harmless worshipers. It became obvious to him that some sort of sacrifice was planned, and he did not know how to stop it.

"He was afraid to go against Duff, and so he and his wife just let it go on. Apparently they had originally planned something else, possibly just the sacrifice of some of the local pets that have been missing, but when that Tyler boy showed up in their camp the other day, and they caught him exploring the cave, it was decided that he would be offered instead. Timmons said he only found out a few minutes before the ceremony that the sacrifice was to be human. Before then, Tyler Roberts had been kept in the Duff's tent and Timmons never saw him.

"It was only when things were happening in the cave, and Timmons finally understood what was going to happen, that he realized that he had to do something to stop it. That's his story, anyway. He claims that he was trying to run out of the cave to get help. Funny that he didn't run for help until Rathbone shot Duff, though."

"How did they find James Wade?" I asked.

"James came following after us last night," said the chief. "He didn't stay with the automobiles like he was supposed to. The guards caught him when he got too close to the bonfire. Luckily, they all just assumed he was a curious boy from the neighborhood, and never thought to ask him if anyone else was with him. I'd hate to think what would have happened if they had known we were in that cave and came in after us."

Holmes theorized that after the sacrifices, Duff, Simmons, and Boyd had intended to flee the area, leaving the other worshipers to be questioned later by the locals regarding the missing boys. This was later confirmed by Boyd, who seemed to have no feeling one way or another about the deaths in which he had been involved, and those which had just been prevented.

Later in the morning, Holmes, Rathbone, Brewer, and I reentered the cavern. Holmes agreed with me that the walls appeared to have been shaped and augmented by man at some distant point in the past. Even with the faint daylight penetrating through the outer entrance into the chamber, and with the light of our torches, the place held an evil aura.

Back in the sunshine, we held a discussion. The chief stated that he could vouch for his men, and that this matter would be kept in strict confidence. "It wouldn't do for the folks around here to realize what has just happened," he said. He indicated that most of the people arrested had probably not realized what they were getting into until the boys were actually brought forward to the sacrificial table. Then, they had been too caught up in the religious frenzy to try and stop it.

Holmes stated, "I suppose that is possible, and there is really no way to prove otherwise. However, for so many Druids to have willingly agreed to greet the sunrise on one of their most important days while deep in a cavern, with no possible view of the sun, indicates to me that they were quite aware of what was going on. As soon as Watson and I saw the Druid death symbol, and learned of the proximity of an underground opening, we both knew that we were dealing with a dark mirror of true Druidism. Surely these people knew it as well, or they would never have agreed to miss the rising of the sun."

Brewer explained that the participants would simply be charged with vagrancy and thrown out of the county. He was certain that none of them would ever return. Duff and his cronies would be charged with attempted murder, but he would work to keep the graphic details of the events from becoming common knowledge.

"I think that it would be best if this place were filled up," said Holmes, gesturing toward the entrance to the chamber. "Locations like this are magnets of evil. You need to prevent something like this from happening again."

The chief agreed, and stated that some of his men would begin immediately to fill the chamber with stone and then blast the entrance, making it impossible to enter. "And I'm sure I can get Mr. Timmons to arrange things so that the aluminum company will pay for any expense, in the name of making this park safer. After all, Timmons probably won't be charged in the matter, either, and he is going to owe me."

Rathbone drove us back to our lodgings at Mrs. Jones's farm. We retired to change out of our dirty clothing, and then returned to the main house to find that Rathbone was engaged in relating our night's adventures to the lady. It was at that moment that Mrs. Jones recognized us, and it was then that she made me promise not to use her actual name, should I ever write a narrative of what had taken place. We agreed, as long as she promised not to reveal what Rathbone had told her.

Later in the day, we checked on Mrs. Wade and James, where we found that he had completely recovered from the incident. In his mind it had already become somewhat dreamlike, and the horror was starting to blur. We told Mrs. Wade some of the less graphic details of the previous night's events, and assured her that the Druids were gone and that the cavern was to be destroyed.

James went to Tyler's house, returning with the small boy in a few minutes. He confirmed that he had been captured by Duff and his men while trying to explore the cavern. He had been aware of the passageway and buried chamber for months, and he wondered what the visiting Druids were doing in it. He thought of the whole thing as a great adventure, and was not traumatized in the least. His parents were not concerned at all for the simple reason that he had not told them of it, and had no intention of doing so.

Back in town, we met with Chief Brewer once again, who informed us that work was already underway to close the ancient underground room. We gave him information on how to reach us with future details regarding the disposition of the case. He looked at our addresses, mine in London and Holmes's in Sussex. "Not 221b Baker Street?" he asked with a grin.

"No," replied Holmes, "not anymore."

The next day, Rathbone delivered us to the train station, where we intended to travel to Knoxville, and from there back to Linville, where we would conclude our business before returning to England.

As we shook his hand, Holmes thanked Rathbone for his assistance. "Think nothing of it, gentleman," he said. "Most fun I've had in years. Too bad that you had that hole filled in, though, Mr. Holmes. I would have liked to have set up a stand and given paid tours through the place. Just think, 'Ladies and gentleman, this way to the amazing Druid Death Cave!' "

We laughed, and Rathbone waved and walked to his cab. Later, as we adjusted to our seats for the short ride to Knoxville, Holmes remarked, "I have enjoyed this little side trip, Watson."

"As did I. By the way, did you ever find any evidence of corruption at the college?"

"None whatsoever. I have been in touch with Mrs. Thaw several times by wire, and I learned that her suspicions arose out of a comment relating to the construction of the new building. Apparently there are some sinkholes beside the proposed location, and the builder indicated that those would have to be 'covered up.' Word reached her, and in her confused elderly state, she misunderstood and believed that the college was involved in a different kind of 'cover-up' relating to the building. From that, she extrapolated the notion that there was some sort of plot afoot to misuse her funds."

I laughed, and said, "Perhaps if we let him know, Rathbone can persuade the college to leave the sinkholes open. It's not quite a Druid horror chamber, but he could still sell admission."

Holmes shook his head with a smile. "An enterprising young fellow, this American cousin of mine. As was your relative, Willie Marcum."

"Yes," I agreed. "We have no reason to worry about our American relations."

"What if, Watson," said Holmes, "what if, someday, Willie were to have a son or daughter, and that person were to marry Rathbone's son or daughter. Then our families, however distant, would be linked."

"I think I would like that, Holmes," I replied. "That would be a fine thing to happen."

The train picked up speed, our first step on the return home. Holmes and I fell into a comfortable silence, each gazing out the window at the beautiful passing landscape.

The Adventure of the Other Brother

With many thanks to Sir Arthur Conan Doyle,
August Derleth, and Rex Stout (the Literary Agents),
and William S. Baring-Gould (a Perceptive Biographer)

PART I: THE OTHER BROTHER

In late October 1896, I had been involved in a series of personal matters that caused me no little distress, as well as the inconvenient requirement that I temporarily move out of our Baker Street lodgings for nearly a week. During that time, I had seen Mr. Sherlock Holmes on a daily basis, as I stopped in to get fresh clothing and linens, as well as to retrieve my mail. As my presence was not always required elsewhere during the daytime hours, I had also accompanied Holmes on several investigations during that time.

On the last day of the month, I had returned to Baker Street for good, my business completed. Although the specific details of the matter have no relation to the present narrative, they did contribute to my mood that day. I was quite grim following a long week of struggles with a patient whose identity must remain anonymous. It was in such a dark attitude that I dropped into my chair in front of the sitting room fire.

Holmes was moving around in his bedroom. I could hear his occasional murmurs as he opened and closed drawers in the bedroom behind me. Soon he came in, and as if noticing the darkness of the room for the first time that afternoon, he stepped to the windows and threw back the drapes.

The weak additional light barely improved the condition of the dark room. Holmes sat in his chair across from me and glanced at my bag standing near the landing door. "It is finished, then?" he asked.

I nodded. "For better or worse."

"I, too, have received word today of some business relating to a painful matter from the past." He tossed me a telegram that had been hidden in his dressing gown pocket.

As I scanned the message, the events of the previous summer came flooding back to me, temporarily pushing aside my despondency over the day's conclusion.

"So he has escaped," I said softly.

"And apparently with no great difficulty. He must have been biding his time. The local constabulary waited far too long before notifying any other authorities. By the time Mycroft became aware of the matter, and was able to bring more skilled forces to bear, it had become apparent that the fugitive had fled across the German sea. . . ."

We were silent for a moment. "Do you think we shall meet him again?" I finally asked.

Holmes reached for his pipe. He did not answer as he went through the process of packing it with the dry shag tobacco from the Persian slipper. Finally, he replied, "Yes, Watson. I do not know how or when, but I very much fear that we shall meet him again."

As we continued to sit in the growing darkness, I recalled the events of half a year earlier. I had been amazed at the time, as well as angry with Holmes for his infernal habit of keeping secrets from me. However, at the conclusion of the case, I had believed that a great wrong had been righted. Now I knew that we would always be waiting to learn when this evil would reappear.

It was on a morning in early June of that same year that we became involved in the affair that I have always called "The Other Brother." I had been in the process of writing up several matters relating to Holmes's activities, including some incidents that took place during his travels for the Foreign Office from 1891-94, when everyone but his brother Mycroft believed him to be dead. Unfortunately, except for certain members of Her Majesty's government, the exact details of these events must remain secret until late into the next century.

Holmes had been involved for several days in a number of cases, including most recently the singularly unrewarding matter of Mr. Josiah Uppenham's tedious financial miscalculations. He was sitting at our dining table, surrounded by numerous stacks of documents, each threatening to slide and spill into its neighbor. At times Holmes would mutter, and lean forward with his head on his hand, squinting at the minuscule purple entries and jottings. Sometimes he would make a note, and other times he would lean back, sigh, and reshuffle and stack the papers a different way, occasionally making a note on a document as some sort of cross-referencing.

I did not know how long this would go on, but I suspected that Holmes would stop soon, if only to relieve the pain he must be feeling in his stooped back. It was into this setting that Mrs. Hudson arrived with a telegram.

Holmes stood, sighed, and stretched with an audible crack from his back. "Watson, I am tempted to let Mr. Uppenham suffer the consequences of his foolishness," he said, opening the wire. "He needs a team of sharp solicitors, not a lone consulting detective with a leery respect at best for mathematics. Luckily I am being generously compensated, in this instance for my reputation, I believe, more than my skills. . . ."

His voice trailed off as he read the telegram. The fatigue seemed to slough from him as he stood taller. He finished reading, looked toward the door for a short moment, and then moved toward his bedroom. Over his shoulder, he stated, "Can you come to Yorkshire today, Watson? Are you available for several days?"

I turned in my desk chair. "Of course," I replied.

He returned to the door, carrying some folded clothing. "Bring your service revolver."

I stood up as he turned back into the bedroom. "What is it, Holmes?"

He called from the other room, "My brother has been arrested for murder."

"What?" I cried. "Mycroft arrested? In Yorkshire?"

"Not Mycroft," he said, reappearing around the doorway. "My older brother, Sherrinford."

Later, as we sat in our compartment on the northbound train, I caught Holmes's eye and asked the obvious question. "You have another brother?"

He looked at me for another moment, and then out the window at the landscape, which began to pass more quickly as we left the sprawl surrounding London.

Earlier, I had grabbed my bag and gun, meeting Holmes on the landing within minutes of his request for my company on the trip. I am an old campaigner, and after years attending Holmes on his investigations, I had learned to always keep a bag ready for immediate departure. We had been silent in the hansom ride to King's Cross, and I could tell that Holmes was in deep thought and would not appreciate being disturbed.

He had, however, at one point silently handed me the telegram that had precipitated this journey. It simply said, "Sherrinford arrested for murder. Compartment booked for you on special train, King's Cross. Information to follow upon your arrival. Mycroft."

Now, in the train, I wanted answers, and knew that we had several hours for Holmes to provide them. "Perhaps," he said, "I should give you a little background information about my family, so that you will know something about them when we arrive." I nodded, and he continued.

"In the fall of 1888," he began, "I believe you were surprised to learn that I had an older brother, Mycroft."

"Surprised is hardly the word," I replied. I still remembered that evening vividly. Holmes and I had been sitting before our fireplace, long periods of companionable silence mixed with random conversation.

Holmes had begun to explain that he believed traits and abilities often ran in families. He had sought to prove this point by saying that his older brother Mycroft possessed even greater deductive skills than did Holmes himself. My amazement at learning of a brother, after having known Holmes for over seven years, had led to our visiting Mycroft at the Diogenes Club, that odd gathering place for the most unclubbable men in London. Before the evening was over we were involved in the strange matter of Mr. Melas, the Greek Interpreter.

"At the time, I had come to believe that you had as little family in England as I," I said.

"I had kept Mycroft's existence a secret for several reasons, not the least of which is my own natural tendency towards a certain reluctance for sharing information unnecessarily. It was not that I did not trust you, Watson. I simply had felt no need up to that point in time to mention Mycroft.

"As I said at the time, Mycroft was employed within the British government. I recall mentioning to you last year, during the matter of the stolen submarine plans, that on occasion Mycroft *is* the British government. Again, I did not distrust you by not mentioning this sooner. It was simply not relevant in 1888 to let you know how important Mycroft's position was and continues to be.

"In 1868, Mycroft graduated from Oxford and obtained a government position through the influence of a family friend. He moved to London, and found lodgings in Montague Street near the British Museum. The building was owned by a distant family relation, and it would in fact be these rooms in which I would reside when I came down to London several years later.

"Of course, given Mycroft's incredible skills at sorting information and perceiving various relationships between facts unnoticed by others, he was soon being consulted by all sorts of departments within the government. It was a natural progression that he would find himself offering opinions on the mysterious activities and motivations of foreign countries and their leaders. During that time, Mycroft was not nearly as sedate as he would later become, and on several occasions he traveled abroad on a number of secret missions, the nature of which he has never revealed, not even to me.

"During this time, I was a young fellow, spending my time alternately between my family's home in Yorkshire and several schools in different parts of England. My family consisted of my father Siger, my mother Violet, my older brother Sherrinford, and his growing family.

"My father was the second son of a country squire, and had spent time serving as an officer in the military in India before being invalided home due to an injury. His older brother lived in Yorkshire as the squire of the estate. During the time my father was traveling home, his older brother had died, and my father arrived on Portsmouth jetty to learn that he had inherited the estate.

"Not long after taking up his position as a country squire, my father met and married my mother, Violet Sherrinford, the daughter of Sir Edward Sherrinford, a not too distant neighbor. My brother Sherrinford was born about a year later, in 1845. Mycroft followed in 1847. I was born in 1854.

"My father was a great bear of a man, loud and with a full black beard. He was strong-willed and highly opinionated, and he knew exactly what he wanted for each of his three sons. Sherrinford, the oldest, was to be educated and then take over the family estate, continuing the line of country squires that had run the place for ages. Mycroft was to attend university as well and then obtain a position within the government.

"Each of my brothers followed my father's plan and ended up where they were supposed to be. For myself, my father had decided that I was to be an engineer. It was with this in mind that he hired a mathematics tutor to get me ready during the summer of 1872. As I have related before, Watson, this tutor was none other than Professor James Moriarty.

"The Professor and I did not get along at all during that time, but I had no idea then how our differences would grow. In later years, as I became aware of a criminal network forming in England, I still had difficulty believing for sure that my former mathematics tutor had become the leader of the vast underworld machine that he himself created. During that long summer before I went away to university, the house was filled with tension as I fought with Moriarty over the need to learn mathematical theorems, which I felt to be irrelevant, and I questioned my father endlessly about whether I really had to become an engineer.

"The only enjoyment that I had during that summer was playing with my young nephew, William, who had been born the previous year. He is a fine lad, much like his father Sherrinford, and even at that young age his intelligence seemed remarkable. He has also always been a wonderfully even-tempered boy, considering that for a portion of his early years he grew up in the same house as my tempestuous father.

"I credit William's wonderful nature to his mother, Roberta, formerly Roberta MacIvor, who had married Sherrinford in 1868. She became like a second mother to me, especially as my own mother was already in failing health at that time.

"In the fall of 1872, I left Yorkshire to attend Oxford. I was not at home during early 1873 when Sherrinford's second son, Bancroft, was born. I did try to stay in contact with the family as often as I could. On several occasions, however, I accepted invitations to visit other homes with friends I had made while away at school. It was during one of these trips with Victor Trevor to Norfolk in the summer of 1874 that I finally realized my future lay not in the field of engineering, but rather in defining and creating the profession of consulting detective." I recalled the matter of which he spoke. I had learned of it in early 1888, following the death of my first wife. I had moved back to Baker Street, and Holmes had begun to tell me some about his past and a few earlier cases as a way to help me forget my grief. I had later chronicled the matter under the title "The *Gloria Scott.*"

"As you might expect, my father was not pleased when I informed him of my decision," Holmes continued, "and he quickly wrote to me, explaining that he would continue to provide funding for me, but that he never wanted to see me again. Thus released from my duties as a student engineer, I traveled to London, moved into the rooms in Montague Street, and promptly enrolled in Cambridge for the fall, feeling that its scientific emphasis might be better suited in order to prepare me for my new calling.

"For several years I alternated between classes at Cambridge and the Montague Street rooms, learning what I could in the classroom, and more practical lessons on the streets of London at other times. During this period, I found what cases that I could, always trying to use each as a way to extrapolate knowledge for my future profession.

"Over the next few years, I attended classes less and less and worked much more often. I began to build a fairly steady practice, and started to believe that I could make a true profession out of my work. I had also managed to arrange an uneasy truce with my father, and I was able to visit my family as frequently as I could get away, which sadly, was not very often. In 1880, as you know, I traveled with a Shakespearean acting company for a good part of the year to various parts of the United States, and so had no contact with them at all for several months.

"It was during this time that Sherrinford's youngest and last son was born. Coincidentally, Watson, he arrived on the twenty-seventh of July, 1880, the same day that you were fighting for your life at Maiwand. After my return to England in August, I traveled briefly to Yorkshire, where I met this nephew for the first time.

"I must say that of Sherrinford's three children, it is this fellow to whom I feel closest. His name is Siger, after his grandfather, and physically he is very much like me. Although all of my brothers and nephews are quite adept in the art of deduction, which does seem to run in the family as I have previously stated, Siger seems to approach the matter more like me than the others. Interestingly, my oldest nephew, William, is much like Sherrinford, warm and intelligent and suited for country life, while the middle son, Bancroft, is in many ways like his uncle Mycroft. He and Mycroft both have that coldly analytical trait that works so well for those involved in government intrigues.

"In fact, Bancroft has been working for several years in Mycroft's department in London, although in a rather strange way. When he completed his studies at university in 1892, Bancroft expressed a desire to follow in Mycroft's footsteps. However, he wanted it made very clear that anything that he accomplished would be on his own merits, and not due to the influence of his uncle Mycroft or the Holmes name. Therefore, when he went to work, he fashioned a different last name for himself, and has used it ever since, preferring that no one there know that he and Mycroft are related.

"Bancroft based his name on a variation of his father's name, Sherrinford, which comes from the old name for a local spot in a stream used for shearing sheep. The area was known as the *shearing ford,* which was later simply pronounced *sherrinford.* Likewise, the name *Mycroft* comes from a similar local derivation, based on an ancestor exclaiming *'My croft!'* Thankfully, I am not aware of any local words or phrases that have been derived or corrupted into *Sherlock.*

"Since his father's name was based on a ford across a stream, Bancroft decided that he would figuratively build a bridge across that stream, instead of using the ford. He initially took the last name *Bridge*, but he decided that he did not like the alliteration of *Bancroft Bridge*, and subsequently changed his pseudonym to the Latin for bridge, *pons.* Bancroft's choice to change his last name and the way he created it are typical of the crafty and, if I may say it, rather twisted way that his and my brother Mycroft's minds work. No doubt this is why they get along so well together, and also the reason for the great success of the department that Mycroft has created.

"As I said, Bancroft went to work in Mycroft's department in 1892, and he was soon placed in charge of managing my activities as I traveled throughout Asia and the Middle East, as well as various locations in Europe and the United States. It was good practice for him, as I understand that he is now fairly in charge of most of Mycroft's field agents, as a good part of Mycroft's time is still spent collecting and arranging data from all departments of the government, not just for the Foreign Office, as well as dealing with politicians and military leaders."

By now, we were quite a distance from London, and the train was moving at a good pace. I could not believe how much information about his past that Holmes had just related to me. I had understood for years that he had no family, and had been amazed years before when I learned about Mycroft. To learn that there were others, parents, a brother and sister-in-law, and three nephews who each strangely mimicked the three older Holmes brothers, was almost too amazing. I did my best not to interrupt, as I did not want Holmes to realize just how much he was revealing and suddenly decide to stop. However, I had to ask one question.

"I still do not understand," I said, "why these people had to remain a secret."

"Ah," said Holmes. "Normally they would not. However, there was an incident which threatened them, and it was felt that a certain . . . separation between the Yorkshire family and their wayward London relations was necessary.

"As I said, Mycroft began to be noticed by the government early on, and his position advanced at a very quick rate. Soon he was helping to evaluate and decide policy for many departments. It was also not long before agents of foreign governments began to hear of this wonderful man whose brain was being used as some sort of human calculating machine.

"To this day, I do not know all the details of what happened. Likewise, Sherrinford's family does not know exactly what threat faced them, only that they were in danger, and Mycroft will not disclose what happened, or what action was taken against the aggressors. All I do know is that in September 1880, just a month after I visited my new nephew Siger, something happened to threaten the family at the Yorkshire home, and it was clearly related somehow to Mycroft's position with the government. Even then, Mycroft's incredible value to the Crown was recognized, and it was decided at the highest levels to prevent anything like that from happening again, so that nothing of the sort could be used against him or to bring pressure on him.

"Members of the village around the family estate were contacted by agents of Her Majesty's government and asked to help give the impression that the Holmes family of North Riding had nothing to do with Mycroft, and me as well. I suppose that even then, I had been of some use on a few matters, and Mycroft included me in the plan, as he knew I would be staying in London and continuing to get into all sorts of trouble with the more questionable elements of society.

"After making sure that the local individuals understood what was required and were willing to cooperate, references to Mycroft, myself, and various other family members were quietly removed from the official records. That is why you will not find a record of me at Oxford, or Cambridge, or at Bart's Hospital. And none of that branch of the Holmes family will be recorded in the local Parish book near our family home.

"It was not a perfect plan, but it was hoped that it would be enough to confuse or stop the actions of an enemy agent trying to use threats against Sherrinford's family to coerce Mycroft or myself. Over the years, neighbors have reported occasional attempts to find out something about our family, sometimes by reporters, at other times by mysterious individuals whom we can only assume have been agents of criminal or foreign organizations.

"Our biggest fear was always some sort of threat from Professor Moriarty or his organization. The man had actually stayed in our house for most of a summer, and he certainly knew where and who we were. However, he never made a move against my family, and I can only assume he had some sort of odd code of honor that prevented him from doing so. Perhaps he felt a sense of obligation due to the fact that he was well treated while he was there. Possibly he thought that I knew something about his own family as well, and he mistakenly believed that I would make a move against them in retaliation. Perhaps I would have. Luckily, he appears to have kept all information about us and the summer that he stayed there to himself, because there has never been any indication that the subsequent individuals who tried to resurrect his criminal web have any clue of our existence."

We pondered these thoughts in silence for a moment, before I said, "You have described your family in Yorkshire as Sherrinford's family. Does this imply that your parents are no longer living?"

"My mother passed away in April 1888. I did not mention the fact to you then, although you were living in Baker Street. In retrospect, the event left me far more shaken than I acknowledged at the time. My father had died much earlier, in the summer of 1877, before he ever had a chance to see that I had managed to make a real success of the career that I had chosen, and that he had ridiculed."

I recalled that spring of 1888. Holmes had never given any indication to me at the time of the death of his mother. Perhaps the only sign of a problem at all was a stumble during a few of his cases, most noticeably the investigation into the mysterious tenant living in the house adjacent to Mr. Grant Munro. It will be recalled that Holmes had theorized a completely incorrect and rather grim solution, and upon learning that the truth was far more pleasant, he had asked me to whisper "Norbury" in his ear if he ever again seemed to be becoming over-confident in his powers, or not taking the proper amount of interest or care in a case.

The train sped on, and we sat in silence for a number of miles, each lost in our own memories. I understood how Holmes felt. My father had died of alcohol poisoning following a wasted life that had spiraled down from success, solidity, and respectability to unbeatable failure. The death of my mother, which occurred much sooner than it should have due to anguish over my father's abandonment, had left me unsettled and grief-stricken. When I was older, after becoming a doctor, I had traveled for a number of years, as well as spent time in the army, coming to grips with the bitter feelings I had retained following my parents' deaths.

I gradually became aware of the train compartment, and Holmes watching me from his seat on the other side. Clearing my throat, I asked, "So now who resides at the family home?"

"Sherrinford and Roberta, their oldest son William, who has not yet married, and Siger, who is about to turn sixteen. I confess I am looking forward to seeing Siger again. It has been a year or so since I visited. The last time was just prior to my return to London in April '94, a day or so after I arrived back on English soil. When I saw him then he was already using the methods of ratiocination in a way far more advanced of my skills when I was at that age."

I laughed. Most people would have commented that the boy was taller than expected, or some such observation. Only Holmes would think in terms of deductive skills. "You still thought that you were going to be an engineer at that age," I said. "An engineer, indeed."

He laughed as well, but just for a moment before the seriousness returned to his expression.

"Do you know anything of Sherrinford's arrest?" I asked.

He shook his head. "Nothing more than what is in that telegram. I assume we will be able to begin our investigation as soon as we arrive. No doubt Mycroft will manage to reach us with any information that he believes we will need."

We continued on northward, each lost in our private thoughts. As for myself, I was still thinking of the wealth of information that I had just received regarding Holmes's background and family life. Holmes's frowning face was pinched in concentration, his pipe — which had long since gone out — clamped in his teeth. Although he made it a practice never to theorize in advance of data, I did not see how he would be able to refrain from some sort of speculation regarding his brother Sherrinford's dilemma. However, I knew he would be unwilling to discuss the matter, and I left him to his thoughts.

PART II: HOME

We changed trains in York for the line to Thirsk. After arriving in that picturesque town, we found seats on a smaller branch line, and I must have slept at some point. When I awoke we were pulling into a tiny village station. Following Holmes's lead, I began to gather my things for departure. We had no sooner stepped onto the platform than a neatly dressed man stepped forward to intercept us.

"Mr. Holmes," he said. "Dr. Watson? I am Inspector Tenley. I have been briefed on the matter, and I will be accompanying you to your family home."

In actuality, Tenley did not say "your family home." Rather, he named the community which was our destination. However, in spite of the passage of years since these events took place, I will not name or identify the location any more specifically than I have already done so. Even though this narrative will be placed in my tin dispatch box following its completion, where it is intended to remain for at least seventy-five years after my death, I am not willing to compromise the security of the Holmes family, or to negate the incredible efforts already made over the years by the British government to shield and protect them.

Tenley led us to a connecting train for the remaining journey to the village in question. The trip was tedious, as we were in a compartment with a stranger, requiring that we make no discussion of the case to pass the time.

Arriving at the village station, Tenley gestured toward the adjacent roadway. "This way, gentlemen," he said. "I have transportation waiting."

Outside, a rugged four-wheeler stood, pulled by a stout and patient horse. Holding the reins was a small, wiry man who looked once at us, then faced forward again without comment. As we found our seats, Tenley said, "This is Griffin. He can be trusted."

Griffin softly snapped the reins and the four-wheeler lurched into motion. "I believe we have time to discuss the details of the case now, Mr. Holmes, if you prefer."

"That will be fine," Holmes said. "We know virtually nothing, as we left London immediately after being notified of the arrest. The charge is murder, then?"

"Yes, sir. No possibility of an accidental death or suicide. Your brother has been very cooperative, but professes to have total ignorance on the matter."

"Pray give me the facts," said Holmes, shifting in his seat toward Tenley.

Tenley watched for a moment as Holmes closed his eyes, so that he might better concentrate on the narrative. "Yesterday morning," Tenley began, "your nephew William arrived at the local police station, quite agitated, requesting that the constable accompany him back to the Holmes farm, where the body of a middle-aged man had just been discovered, brutally murdered.

"The officer, Constable Worth, quickly joined William, who drove them in a carriage the five miles or so out to the house. Upon entering the estate, they bypassed the house and adjacent farm buildings, driving out into a pasture several hundred feet away. The area is rock-bound, and has many low and hidden areas created by the steeply rolling hills."

"The north pasture," Holmes said, without opening his eyes. "Go on."

"The entire area has been used for sheep grazing, as I'm sure you know," continued Tenley. "William drove the carriage around a number of rocky areas until they reached a low spot, surrounded by several farm hands and your brother Sherrinford.

"Upon reaching their destination, Worth jumped down and advanced through the ring of silent men, all staring at something below them. The location is a natural pit in the earth, an inverted cone some eight or ten feet deep, and whatever is in it would be quite hidden below the view of anyone on the surrounding pasture. I was told that during times of heavy rain, the pit fills with water before it gradually seeps away into the ground. We have had no rain, however, for several weeks, and at the time of the murder, it was dry. Although," he said, glancing at the sky, "I suspect we are due for some rain shortly."

"I know of the place you speak," said Holmes. "I used to camp there as a small boy."

Tenley nodded, unnoticed by Holmes. "At the bottom of the pit was the body of the victim, a fellow in his early fifties. He was lying on his back, and had apparently only been there a few hours, as there was no sign of disturbance of the corpse by birds or animals.

"Constable Worth questioned your brother, Sherrinford, who told him that William discovered the body that morning. While walking toward a distant field, he had happened to glance into the pit as he skirted its edge. Upon seeing the body, he rushed down and ascertained that the man was dead. He then returned to the house, where he informed his father. By that time, a number of farmhands had gathered around them. Sherrinford sent William for the police, saying that he and the hands would guard the body until William returned. Sherrinford then walked to the body's location with the other men. He made sure that no one approached the body while they awaited the constable's arrival. He stated that he was aware, Mr. Holmes, of the need to preserve the area around the body.

"Constable Worth is a capable man, a typical rural official and quite observant in his own way. He made a cursory examination of the area. He did not see any signs of footprints or disturbances around the body, although as I have said, we have had no rain for several weeks, and it is unlikely that anything would show on the ground. Worth was unable to even see any of William's footprints at the immediate site, or any of his own, for that matter.

"The body had a great torn cut on the throat, but strangely there was very little blood around that wound or on the collar of the man's suit. There was more blood on the man's back that had soaked through the coat, but a quick examination by Worth did not reveal the nature of that wound. Also, Worth reported that there was very little blood on the ground below the body. I have since verified this, as well as Worth's conclusion that no footprints were detectable in the hollow. It seems, based on the evidence of the blood, that the fellow was murdered elsewhere and the body was placed there after the fact.

"Worth immediately recognized the murdered man, and asked Sherrinford if he knew who it was, as well. 'Of course,' replied Sherrinford. 'We all know him. It is Davison Wilkies. I have given him and his people permission to camp on my land. They have been here for a week or so.'

"This agreed with Worth's knowledge of the situation. Wilkies was the leader of a group of a dozen or so odd folk, apparently part of some self-styled religious cult. They had arrived in the area about ten days ago, like a band of gypsies, all traveling in six or eight large wagons pulled by heavy teams of horses. Your brother had given them permission to stay on the Holmes land, although he directed them to the southern side, where the fields are much flatter and more hospitable, and there is access to water from the stream.

"It was common knowledge that Sherrinford had visited with Wilkies at the campsite on a number of occasions, usually in the evening. Your brother stated that he was curious about the group's beliefs, and that he was simply going to see Wilkies in order to ask questions. We learned this from both Sherrinford, as well as from Wilkies's daughter, Sophia.

"Sophia indicated that on the night of the murder, Wednesday night, your brother visited Wilkies's wagon, as usual. She states that while she did not hear the exact conversation, the tone between the two men became tense, and then somewhat hostile. They appeared to be arguing regarding the nature and validity of Wilkies's beliefs. Sophia indicated that Sherrinford appeared to be of the opinion that Wilkies had turned away from the 'true path,' whatever that means. Sherrinford denies that this conversation ever took place, and states that his visit that night was cordial, and no different than those of other nights. He also does not even know what was meant by the phrase 'true path,' since he was only a curious and casual visitor with little knowledge of Wilkies's beliefs.

"No one else in the campsite can be found to verify or disprove either of their statements. However, Sophia said that she doubted if anyone else would have overhead the conversation. Although she says that the two men were disagreeing quite strongly, they were quiet about it, and even though Sophia overheard some of the conversation from her location immediately outside the wagon, she does not believe the voices would have carried any farther.

"Sophia initially related this information to Constable Worth, when he questioned her yesterday morning following the notification of her father's death. When asked who might have had a reason to kill her father, she could think of no one, with the exception of your brother, whom she stated had argued with her father the night before. She indicated that the group did not know anyone else in the area, and that no one within her group would have had any reason for murdering her father.

"She also did not know how her father's body could have come to be located so far away from the campsite. Wilkies's party is quite a distance to the south of the house, while the rocky area where he was discovered is to the north. Constable Worth's investigations did not show any signs of blood in the campsite, indicating that he was not murdered there, and my subsequent examination confirmed this.

"Based on Sophia's statement, Worth returned to the Holmes farm, where he made a surreptitious examination of the grounds and outbuildings. In one of the barns, he thought that he found something of interest, a bundle of old clothing, consisting of an old shirt, the sleeves covered in blood and gore. However, subsequent investigation revealed this to be simply an old shirt belonging to one of the farm workers, used in the past during butchering time. However, based on the evidence of Sophia's story, Worth felt that he had no choice but to arrest Sherrinford.

"It is Worth's belief that Wilkies and Sherrinford must have known each other at some time in the past, although Sherrinford denies it. Worth feels that Wilkies did not just come to this area by chance, and that he was actually invited here by Sherrinford, who let him stay on the Holmes property because of their past relation. They must have both been members of the same religious belief at some point in the past, but Wilkies has changed or modified his beliefs. Sherrinford was dismayed upon learning that Wilkies no longer followed the 'true path,' and this turned to anger, which led to Wilkies's murder.

"Worth believes that Sherrinford lured Wilkies to some spot Wednesday night, where he killed him, before concealing the body in the hollow. He intended to return and bury it the next night, but it was discovered by William before he was able do so. He then had to play along. Worth has not yet found where Wilkies was killed, but he is still looking. Obviously, wherever the murder took place, a great deal of blood will have been spilled, and there is no sign of this in any of the farm buildings or on locations immediately near them. It is Worth's contention that Sherrinford hid his own bloody clothing and knife, having changed following the murder. He meant to bury them with the body, but he never got the chance. He hid the body in the dark following the murder, not realizing that it would be visible when that area was in daylight.

"As I said, Mr. Holmes, this is Constable Worth's contention. He did investigate the likelihood of any other possibility all yesterday, but by late evening he had no choice but to arrest your brother. As of right now, we have found no evidence to the contrary, so I have allowed Worth's arrest of your brother to stand. However, I am interested in finding all the facts in order to get at the truth.

"Following Sherrinford's arrest, his family, of course, wasted no time in contacting London. Within hours, I was assigned to the case. I came out with Worth this morning, and we reexamined the hollow where the body was found, and spoke with both your brother and Sophia. I reported directly to your brother, Mycroft, in London. He informed me that you would be arriving soon to investigate as well."

Holmes opened his eyes. "Is Sherrinford being held in the village, or in the facilities of some larger town?"

"In the village," Tenley replied. "Worth is rather ambitious, and he seemed to want to keep the matter within his own sphere of influence. He had made no effort on his own to call for any assistance, believing that he was handling the case sufficiently by himself. He was in fact somewhat resentful when your family arranged for my participation."

Tenley added, "As I said, Mr. Holmes, Worth is quite competent and observant, but also ambitious. I will be watching to make sure that his ambition does not cloud his judgment."

"Quite," replied Holmes. "And the body? Is it also still in the village?"

"Yes," replied Tenley. "Worth requested an autopsy this morning, but I stopped it until you could be here to examine the body first."

"Excellent," said Holmes. "Who will be doing the autopsy?"

"Dr. Dalton," said Tenley.

Holmes smiled tightly. "As I supposed."

"Do you wish to see the body first, or go on to the site of its discovery?" Tenley asked.

Holmes glanced at the low clouds. The wind had picked up somewhat since we had left the train station, and the air was noticeably cooler. I agreed with Tenley's earlier observation about the imminent arrival of rain.

"I suppose we should see the hollow first," said Holmes, "although I am sure that you are correct and that very little will be discovered."

Tenley instructed Griffin to continue on to the farm. We rode in silence, Tenley and Holmes both wrapped in their own thoughts, while I looked from side to side at the surrounding fields and copses, examining with interest that area from which Holmes had sprung. I tried to imagine him as a boy, with his great and curious intellect, roaming and exploring this countryside. It was difficult, to say the least. Holmes had always been comfortable and competent in all situations, but I generally thought of him as a man of the city. However, I also knew that he had showed a familiarity with country life, including knowledgeable experience with horses, and that living once in a rude stone hut on the wilds of Dartmoor had not seemed to cause him any serious distress. Obviously, he had gathered these and other skills here, as a boy.

We topped a low rise, and spread out before us was a tidy manor house, surrounded by a cluster of barns and smaller farm buildings. The house was unostentatious but well kept. On several sides were fenced paddocks, and the fence rails were brightly whitewashed. The ground around the buildings was flat and trim, and stretched away smoothly to the south. Behind the house, beyond the trees obviously planted as windbreaks, the land changed, turning rocky and rippled toward the north. I knew that this was the area where the body was found. "What is in that direction?" I asked, gesturing toward the rocky piles.

"Nothing," said Holmes. "Eventually one would run into the German Sea. The ground stays jumbled that way for a number of miles before flattening out on a high, rough tableland. There are a few shepherd cottages scattered out there. I suppose that is where William was going yesterday morning when he discovered the body."

"That is correct, Mr. Holmes," said Tenley. "He was going to take a message to one of the men out there, asking him to drive the sheep back toward the main house. Your brother says he wanted to examine them to make sure there were no signs of any infectious disease in the flock. There had been reports of something going through farms in nearby towns."

As we approached the house, the front door opened, and two men and a woman stepped out. Two or three farmhands also moved into the darkening daylight from a nearby barn. They stayed there, in the doorway, while the people from the house moved closer to us. The four-wheeler stopped, and the woman walked to the side.

"Sherlock," she said. "Thank you for coming." Holmes stepped down, and the woman reached and drew him into a hug. Holmes looked mildly uncomfortable for a moment, and then relented to the woman, hugging her back.

I looked at the woman, assuming that this was Roberta, whom Holmes had said was like a second mother to him. She was short, not much over five feet in height, with thick brown hair pulled back into a loose bun. The hair was somewhat shot with gray, but it only added to her commanding and confident

101

presence. "Why have you waited so long to visit?" she asked. "It shouldn't have taken something like this to get you up here."

She turned to me. "And you must be Dr. Watson," she said, shaking my hand with a firm and warm two-handed grip. There was no pretense of delicate lady-like behavior here. She was a woman of the country, strong and not uncomfortable about showing it. "I am Roberta Holmes. I'm so happy to finally meet you, and sorry that it has taken this long to do so," she said, glancing at Holmes with scolding eyes. "You have no idea how many times I have told Sherlock to invite you. It has been nearly impossible, however, to even get *him* to visit . . . . "

While she had been speaking, the older of the two young men behind her stepped forward, his hand outstretched toward Holmes. "Uncle," he said. "I'm very glad that you're here."

Holmes returned his handshake. "William," he said. "It has been too long."

William was a tall, solid fellow in his mid-twenties. He was more heavily built than Holmes had been at that age, although not nearly as portly as his uncle Mycroft. His face clearly showed the Holmes family features, including a high hairline, aquiline nose, and piercing gray eyes. He was dressed in work clothes, and when he turned and shook my hand, I could feel the rough calluses on his palms.

Holmes turned to face the second young man, a thin fellow who was the spitting image of a young Sherlock Holmes. Tall, perhaps an inch taller even than Holmes, with Holmes's same sharp gaze and precise movements. I knew that he was nearly sixteen, but he seemed much older. He was not dressed for farm work. Rather, he was in more casual clothing, as if our arrival had interrupted his studies. He stuck out his hand, which Holmes grasped and shook.

"Siger," he cried. "Your mother wrote that you had grown, but I did not realize how much so. How have you been?"

"Tolerable," Siger replied. "I will be better when I can get down to London."

"Siger," his mother interrupted, with a warning tone. "This is not the time to start that, with our visitors just setting foot on the place." She turned to us. "You'll hear all about it before you go, but life on the farm is not going to satisfy Siger, here. He has heard too much of London from his brother Bancroft, as well as what he has gleaned over the years from you, Sherlock, and Mycroft, and your writings, Dr. Watson."

Siger turned in my direction. "Ah, Dr. Watson, we finally meet." He shook my hand, and then said, "You have been in Thirsk, I perceive."

Then he laughed in a peculiar silent way. I had only ever heard one other person laugh that way: Sherlock Holmes.

I smiled, recognizing the source of Siger's joke, but Roberta said, sternly, "None of that smart tongue of yours, Siger." Turning to me, she apologized. "He reads too much, I think, doctor."

"Not at all, mother," said Siger. "Of course he's been in Thirsk. They just arrived here on the train. But I didn't just assume it and accept it. I *verified* it." He pointed to my shoes, which had a grayish mud clinging to the instep. "That mud is only at one location around here. It is from the side yard at the Thirsk station, where the coal dust and crushed clinker mixes with the local soil to form this distinctive gray material. There has been no rain for several days, so obviously the doctor walked through a damp spot of that particular mud while getting to their vehicle. There is some of it on the floor of the four-wheeler there, where the doctor was sitting. It has obviously fallen off of his shoes.

"It isn't enough to assume that they came from Thirsk simply because we knew their approximate arrival time and also that Thirsk has the closest major train station. I was able to verify it by observing the mud and relating it to the assumption. Isn't that the correct way to do it, Uncle?" Siger concluded, turning to Holmes.

"Exactly right," answered Holmes. "You are learning. Keep it up. There will be a place for you in London if you do."

"Don't go filling his head full of *that*," said Roberta. "He's going to university in a year or so, and that's that."

"Be careful of whom you hire as a math tutor," Holmes muttered softly, so that only I could hear.

Roberta turned toward the house. "Now come inside and have something to eat or drink, and let's talk about why you're here. I'm sure you'll want to examine things, and I know Sherrinford is looking forward to speaking with you."

"I'm afraid we cannot join you inside just yet," said Holmes. "We must get out to the pit where the body was found before the rains come."

All eyes glanced skyward. The wind was picking up, and sighing through the nearby windbreak. Hanging from one of the eaves of the house was a set of wind chimes, tolling anxiously.

"Of course," said Roberta. "We will be here when you return."

"May I go with them, mother?" asked Siger eagerly, seeing that William had moved to join us.

Roberta smiled with tolerant affection. "Yes, but try to leave something for your uncle to solve, won't you?"

As she returned to the house, we climbed back into the four-wheeler with Griffin, who turned the horse and drove us out of the yard. Passing several of the outbuildings, we were observed by the farmhands who had come out to watch our arrival. They nodded in our direction, and then returned inside to their tasks.

As we passed the trees, the wind hit us full on, carrying with it a strong indication of impending rain. Siger shifted in his seat to face me.

"When will you be publishing some more narratives of my uncle's cases, Dr. Watson?" he asked.

I glanced at Holmes, whose mouth tightened in irritation, although conversely his eyes crinkled in suppressed humor. "I am currently . . . prohibited from making public any of the records of Holmes's investigations."

"And it shall remain that way," added Holmes. "Perhaps someday, when I am retired, I will write an extended monograph detailing my methods and how they were applied in specific instances. However, they will be published in a single volume encompassing the whole art of detection, and not as romanticized segments in a throw-away magazine."

Inspector Tenley caught my eye with an amused smile. I shrugged.

Siger, however, did not appear to notice, as he was looking at his uncle with some shock. "I am sure that I cannot wait until you have retired to hear more of your adventures," he said. "I have attempted to make use of Dr. Watson's narratives as something of a guide for my own studies, and frankly I need more information. Two dozen narratives do not provide enough data for well-rounded instruction. And besides," he added, with a grin, "I don't even know the real story of why you allowed us to believe you were dead for three years, what you were doing while you were gone, and how you managed to come back. When I have asked Bancroft, he simply informs me that I am too young. Typical Bancroft bluster."

"Most people do not know the story of Holmes's journey and subsequent return," I said. "He has refused to allow me to publish it. In the meantime, his practice has increased substantially over what it was before his hiatus, and many of the clients indicate that it is because they became aware of Holmes through my writings."

"And how many of them express surprise that I am a real person, and not some fictional creation in a storyteller's tale?" asked Holmes acidly.

"You cannot blame me for that," I said. "It was your brother, Mycroft, who managed to spread the word during your supposed 'death' that you were a fictional character, no doubt in order to aid some scheme of his while you carried out his tasks during your disappearance."

Siger leaned forward intently, and I realized that I might possibly be on the verge of revealing too much of Holmes's activities during his travels. Holmes, seeing that I needed a way to escape from this path of the conversation, said, "Siger, if you are serious about following in my footsteps, take my advice. Do not let the facts of your cases be placed into narrative form, giving the majority of the public the impression that you were created by a doctor with too much time on his hands." Seeing the somewhat hurt expression on my face, he added, "However, if you are able to find a doctor who is of invaluable assistance both in your work and as a friend, I highly recommend it."

Feeling somewhat mollified, I looked around me as the four-wheeler slowed to a halt. We were near a rocky outcropping, sprawled around a hollow in the ground before it. We climbed down and walked to it. Only when we were at the edge were we able to see into the bottom of the pit.

It was about fifteen feet across and eight feet deep, with steeply sloping sides. The bottom was irregular, pierced in several areas by boulders sticking up out of the ground. At the top, there was a path running along the front side, opposite the rocky outcropping. It lay quite close to the edge of the pit, so that someone walking on it would have no trouble seeing what lay at the bottom. Even from a few feet further away, however, the contents of the pit would be hidden.

"Where was the body?" asked Holmes, looking about on the path.

"On the front side of the pit," said Tenley, "directly below the trail. Still, it might have remained unseen if William here hadn't looked in while he was walking by."

"It is a regular thing when I pass this way, to make sure that no sheep have fallen in," added William.

Holmes moved several feet up and down the trail. "Nothing left here," he said. "Too many people have passed this way, beginning with William, and then Sherrinford and the farm hands standing here to guard the body." He moved along the edge of the pit, back to where the rocky outcropping behind it began to rise. Then he climbed down, choosing that spot to enter so that he would not disturb where the body had rested.

William watched the darkening clouds, while Siger followed his uncle's actions with a hawk-like intensity. He stepped to rim of the pit, but away from where the body would have been placed, somehow instinctively knowing where he should stand so as not to impede his uncle's investigation.

106

In the hole, Holmes moved back and forth across the bottom, bent nearly double so that his eyes were close to the ground. In a moment he called, "How did the body lie?"

Tenley replied, "He was sitting up with his back against the wall of the pit, right under the trail side so that he wouldn't be seen unless you were standing right on the edge, looking down. The arms were tucked in around him. He was obviously placed in that way intentionally after he was rolled in."

Holmes's examination of the bottom only lasted a further few minutes. As he climbed back out, the first drops of heavy rain began to fall around us. "You were correct, Inspector. There is no blood here. The man was killed elsewhere and brought later." He looked up at the sky, they pulled his cap tighter. "We can learn nothing else here. We'd better get back to the house."

We climbed into the four-wheeler, which Griffin immediately set into motion, moving at a faster pace than when we had traveled out to the pit.

The rain began to fall harder, and we huddled into our coats. Siger had not brought a coat or hat, and was somewhat more miserable than the rest of us. Looking at Holmes's fore-and-aft cap, he stated, "That hat would surely be useful right about now. I'm going to get one of those."

Holmes smiled. "I can tell you, it is a fine item for the country, but I often get odd looks in the city." He gestured over his shoulder. "It is not much further to the house." Soon, we arrived, and the lights of the building and smell of wood smoke made the place seem very inviting indeed.

Inside, the house was warm and pleasant, with the lingering smell of a baked dessert. Roberta asked if we wanted a full meal, but we declined. Roberta insisted that we partake of something. Soon we were seated around a large table as she cut a large iced cake, which had been made that morning. "You seem to be holding up very well," said Holmes, his voice cutting across the muted conversations, "considering the fact that a little over a day ago, a murdered man was found nearby, and your husband arrested."

The people in the room fell silent, and Roberta paused for an almost unnoticed second before she resumed cutting the cake. Passing a filled plate around the table, she answered, "Of course I'm calm. This is all a terrible mistake, and it will soon be sorted out."

We ate for a moment, although none of the conversation resumed.

Suddenly, a knock at the front door made us all look at one another. We heard the front door open, followed by quiet conversation. Then an elderly woman, a member of the household staff, stepped into the room.

"Mr. Augustus Morland is here, ma'am," she said.

Before Roberta could reply, a man appeared in the doorway behind the old woman, who looked back and forth between him and her mistress in a flustered way. The man handed his rain-soaked outer garment to the woman, who took it automatically. "That's all right, Hilda," said Roberta, moving across the room and patting the woman on the shoulder. "Go on back to the kitchen." Turning to the man, her voice grew flat and less friendly, as she said, "What can we do for you, Mr. Morland?"

The man was in his late forties or early fifties, well dressed, and with somewhat long hair combed down beside his thin face. He stood there with a posed arrogance, looking around the room and examining each of us quickly but dismissively. When he looked at me, I could see that his eyes were an odd light brown, and the whites around the pupils were discolored and bloodshot, giving the impression that each entire eyeball was one solid muddy marble. His nose was large and red, covered with tiny broken capillaries that extended out onto his lined red cheeks. In a few seconds, his expressionless gaze at me moved on, but in that short space of time, I felt that he had judged me and found me to be useless.

"I'm sorry to disturb you," he said, his voice strangely high-pitched and staccato. "I simply wanted to stop by and see if there was any help that I could provide."

"Thank you, no," replied Roberta. "We appreciate the gesture. I would offer you some cake, but as you can see, we are having a family meeting with Inspector Tenley here," she said, gesturing toward the inspector, who nodded, "and our discussions are confidential."

"Of course, of course," Morland said. "But before I go, I would like to take a moment to introduce myself to Mr. Holmes." He turned to Holmes. "I was speaking to Constable Worth earlier, and he told me that you were expected in today to look into the matter." He stepped forward, his hand outstretched. "Augustus Morland. Pleased to meet you."

Holmes rose and returned the handshake. Nodding toward me, he said, "This is my associate, Dr. John Watson."

I rose as well, extending my hand, but Morland barely glanced my way. "Yes, of course. I assumed he would be here as well." He moved back toward the door. "Well, I will be going, but as I said, if there is anything that I can do to help during this time, do not hesitate to let me know."

With that, he stepped out of the room, followed by Roberta, who led him to the front door. As she shut it behind him, Tenley said, "Well, what do you suppose was the purpose of that?"

"Not actually an offer to help, I'll wager," said William.

Roberta returned to the room, scowling. "That man!" She said. "You can bet that he is probably enjoying this."

"How do you mean?" asked Holmes.

"Because he's been pressuring father to sell the place," said Siger, sitting forward on his chair.

"Now, Siger," began his mother, but he interrupted her.

"It's true. Just because you haven't chosen to tell me about it, doesn't mean that I didn't know. He's some rich man from Manchester who moved here last year, bought up several of the old farms, and keeps trying to acquire more. He has talked to father several times about buying this place, but father has always turned him down." Roberta shook her head and sat down. "I can see that you've been eavesdropping when we thought you were studying, young man."

"That's not all," continued Siger, without any sign of contrition. "Like William said, he didn't come here to offer help. He wanted to let us know that he knew about our affairs, and that

109

he was receiving information from Constable Worth. I'll bet that Uncle Sherlock's arrival this morning and involvement in the investigation was supposed to remain confidential, was it not, Inspector Tenley?"

Tenley nodded. "It was. You can be certain that I will be speaking to Worth about this."

Holmes spoke to Roberta. "Tell me more about Morland's offers for the property."

"As Siger said," she replied, "the man moved here late last year. His agents had already purchased a couple of adjacent farms before his arrival, and he moved into the larger of the farmhouses when he got here. He is supposedly very wealthy, and there's talk that he may be knighted soon. Within weeks of his arrival, he had purchased several additional holdings, some that had been in families for countless generations, by making huge offers that they couldn't refuse. He's bought one or two more since then, but he has slowed down somewhat. His time has been taken up with other activities, as he has begun building a huge house, a mile or so from the one where he currently resides.

"Not long after arriving here, he visited Sherrinford one day, arriving in the late afternoon. He introduced himself out in the yard, by the big barn, and declined an offer to come inside. Instead, he jumped right to the point, saying he had decided to buy this farm. Sherrinford said that Morland put it as if the place had already been for sale and he was doing us some kind of favor by taking it off our hands. He then named a ridiculously high sum and asked when the matter could be settled legally.

"Sherrinford simply laughed, and explained that the place wasn't for sale. Sherrinford told me that Morland looked at him for a minute, in that curious way you just saw, and then said, 'Everything is for sale. If money doesn't interest you, perhaps you can be persuaded another way.'

"He turned and left that day, but he has been back several times since, increasing his original offer, and becoming more and more frustrated when we kept turning him down."

"And you say he's from Manchester?" Holmes asked Siger.

Siger nodded. "I haven't been able to determine yet how he made his money."

" 'Determine yet'?" his mother said. "Have you been investigating the man?"

"Of course," replied Siger. "As much as I could, anyway. I've asked around the village, and in Thirsk as well, when I've gone there. He has had a number of visitors at his home, all passing through the village. None have Manchester accents. He also receives a lot of telegrams from Manchester and London."

"And how do you know that?" asked Roberta.

"I questioned people," Siger replied. "I considered contacting Bancroft in London, but I decided that he would simply have turned around and let you and father know what I was doing. I would have been able to find out more," he added, "if I had access to better sources of information, and if I was not trapped out here in the middle of nowhere."

William laughed at this statement, and Holmes looked proudly at his young nephew. Roberta threw up her hands in mock despair, before laughing herself, although rather ruefully.

PART III: GATHERING INFORMATION

After another twenty minutes or so, I could see that Holmes was getting restless. Finally he announced that it was time to return to the village, where the autopsy was being delayed until Holmes could examine the body. "Dr. Dalton will not appreciate it if we wait any longer."

We stood and went to the front door, where we began to put on our damp coats. Only after a moment did I realize that Siger had prepared for departure as well. I caught his mother's eye. She smiled and turned her head, as if to accept what she could not change.

Outside, the rain had slackened, and Griffin drove out of the barn, where he had been watching for us.

The drive back into the village passed without conversation. We were soon at a tidy stone house, well kept, with a small sign informing us that we were at Dr. Dalton's surgery. We were

111

arriving well past consulting hours, but in this case it did not matter.

A knock on the door was followed by footsteps echoing across the floorboards inside, and in a moment the door flew open to reveal a man in his early forties, lit from behind by several bright lanterns. He was in his shirtsleeves and waistcoat, and his hair was somewhat long and curly, dancing in the light.

"Come in, come in," he said, moving aside and gesturing for us to enter. "I saw you go by hours ago, thought you might stop then, certainly expected you back before now."

We entered the waiting room, which had apparently once been the front parlor of the house, and removed our coats and hats, which our host set about hanging up. I was able to observe him better, and I could see that he was well built and over six feet in height. He had a weathered face, most notably marked by a strong square chin. There were lines around his eyes, but they seemed more likely to have been formed by years of squinting in the outdoor sunshine rather than from laughter. He shook Tenley's hand, and then mine after Tenley's mumbled introduction. He nodded at Siger and William, and then turned to Holmes.

"Well, well," he said. "The prodigal returns."

Holmes returned his gaze for a silent moment, before remarking, "Wesley. It has been too long."

"Yes, it has. Long enough for you to have died, and then returned."

He gave a short bark of a laugh and stuck out his hand. "Welcome back, Sherlock."

They shook hands, and the tension which I had felt since we entered the home seemed to change somewhat, although it did not entirely abate.

Dalton stepped back, and his face took on a peevish air. "I have really delayed my duties long enough. Are you here to make your examination of the body so that I may proceed with the official one?"

"Certainly," said Holmes. "Please lead the way."

112

Dr. Dalton took us back through a short hallway, into an examining room. Over his shoulder, he remarked to me, "I live upstairs, and the housekeeper has the run of the kitchen at the back of the house. The rest of the ground floor is given over to my practice. We are going to my laboratory, which is set up along one side of the building.

As he finished speaking, we entered a small room, obviously at some time in the past designed to be a ground floor bedroom. Now its walls were covered with shelves containing books, chemicals, and scientific apparatus. In the center of the room was an examination table, upon which lay the body of the dead man, unclothed except for a sheet draped across it.

"As the local coroner," Dalton said, "I am occasionally called upon to conduct autopsies on unfortunate individuals."

Holmes ignored him, stepping closer to the body. I followed, while Siger moved along the other side of the table, showing no signs whatsoever of squeamishness or timidity in the presence of violent death.

The victim was a heavy-set man in his fifties, his head covered in a still-thick toss of grey hair. His face was covered with a thick beard and mustache, both quite unkempt, with the untrimmed beard climbing his cheeks halfway to his eyes. His nose was broad, and appeared to have been broken at some point in the distant past. His eyebrows were a tangled thicket, jutting up from the broad shelf of his forehead like a hedge across his face, running unbroken from side to side.

All of this, however, was secondary to the most noticeable characteristic of the man; namely, a wide puckered gash running across his throat.

"You say that there was very little bleeding from the throat wound?" asked Holmes.

"That is right," said Tenley. "The man's collar and clothing were hardly stained. The wound must have occurred after death."

"The killer was right-handed," interrupted Siger, leaning closely over the gaping opening.

"Correct," said Holmes. "And his throat was cut by someone standing in front of him."

I leaned in and confirmed their conclusions, noticing where the initial tear on the right side of the man's throat was hesitant and somewhat ripped before becoming a clean slice that moved slightly upward toward his left.

"How can you tell that it wasn't caused by a left-handed man standing behind him and reaching across before drawing the weapon back?" asked William.

"The direction of the slash, upward as the blade moved from Wilkies's right to his left, indicates that the killer was moving his arm in that direction while standing in front of him, and that it would have been in the killer's right hand. A man cutting from behind would have most likely pulled the blade in a downward path. Here," said Holmes, moving behind Dalton, "let me show you."

He stepped behind the doctor, and then placed his left arm around the doctor's chest, so that his left hand rested on Dalton's right shoulder.

"Now," he said, "the blade makes initial contact with the throat on the victim's right side, causing a rip before the actual clean slice begins."

He began to pull his hand slowly from his right to left, across Dalton's upper chest. "As you can see, my hand, which would have been holding the blade, drops as it moves across your throat. It would be awkward to pull the blade in an upward direction as it crosses."

"And," said Siger, stepping up to Dalton from the front, "if I were to slash you from the front," he said, crossing his arm so that his right hand was over Dalton's right shoulder, "my hand makes the initial cut in the same place, but as my knife hand, the right hand, moves across your throat, it tends to swing up, as so." And he proceeded to demonstrate, to Dalton's discomfort.

"Yes, yes, thank you very much," he said, pulling himself loose from Holmes and out from underneath Siger's imaginary knife. "However, I'm not sure what difference it makes. Most people are right-handed, you know."

"Yes, but if we encounter a left-handed suspect, it will be something else to weigh in the balance while we consider him," replied Holmes. "Or her." He turned, and resumed his examination of the body. He muttered to himself as he turned the sheet down, peering at the corpse through his lens. Then, with the help of Siger and myself, he rolled the body, and examined the massive wound in the fellow's back.

"Most of the blood on his clothing was from the back wound, you say?" Holmes asked.

"That's right," Dalton confirmed.

"May I see the clothing?"

"Certainly, although I examined it myself. There is nothing in the pockets to give any indication of the murderer's identity. In fact, the pockets were completely empty."

"Nevertheless," said Holmes, taking the bloody bundle from Dalton.

In spite of Dalton's statement, Holmes proceeded to examine the clothing carefully, beginning first with a minute examination of the pockets. As expected, there was nothing in them, not even any lint.

Finally, Holmes shook out the clothes and laid them across the body. Turning them this way and that, he finally said, "Hello, what's this?"

"What?" asked Dalton, although Holmes ignored him.

"Siger," said Holmes, "see if you notice anything."

Siger examined the clothing for less than a minute before announcing, "Wilkies was not wearing these clothes when he was killed."

"*What!*" exclaimed Dalton. Tenley and I were silent. Tenley was watching intently, and I had been around Holmes for too long to be surprised. Holmes nodded for Siger to continue.

"It is obvious that the throat wound was committed sometime after death, due to the lack of bleeding from that site, and that death would have been immediate from the large stab wound in the back, correct?"

"Correct," said Dalton. "The back wound went straight through the heart, and in fact it appears that the knife was rotated and twisted within the body, as if to cause the maximum amount of immediate damage."

"This would appear to be confirmed by the vast amounts of blood on the back of the man's shirt and coat?" continued Siger.

"Yes," said Dalton, with a wary tone. "A wound of that sort would produce copious amounts of blood."

"Then we must ask ourselves," said Siger, warming to his speech, "why the man's shirt and coat, which are both soaked in blood, have no rip or tear in them whatsoever which would have allowed passage of the knife through them and into Wilkies's back?"

"Let me see that!" Dalton said, stepping forward. He leaned in, and then began lifting the clothing to the light. It was obvious that the shirt and coat were whole, and even though the backs of both garments were crusted with blood, there were no holes in the fabrics.

"What does it mean?" asked Dalton.

"Simply that, for reasons unknown to us at this time, Wilkies was killed by a vicious blow to the back. He was either wearing something else at the time, or perhaps entirely unclothed, although this seems less likely to me. Soon after death, the clothes were changed. The wound was still fresh, and so large that a great deal of blood continued to spill from it, staining the clothing. Some time later, after the bleeding had completely stopped, the throat was cut, possibly after Wilkies was propped at the side of the pit."

"But doesn't that invalidate all your evidence about a right-handed man standing in front of him?" asked Dalton.

"Exactly the opposite," replied Holmes. "If the body was propped up and then the killer slashed it, probably to add further evidence of violence, or to complete some ritual, the cut would travel up and to Wilkies's left, as I have theorized. If the killer then stood in the pit, held Wilkies's head back by the hair, and slashed up and to the right, it would be exactly as I have surmised."

Dalton looked irritated. Refolding the clothing, he said, "I would have noticed the lack of cuts in the garments myself, eventually." Placing them on a shelf, he turned back to us. "After

116

all, I have been prevented from carrying out the full autopsy as I have been waiting for your arrival."

Holmes smiled. "Then by all means, Wesley, let us not delay you for another moment. Please let me know of any other information you discover." Then he turned to go. Tenley and I stayed to shake hands with Dalton, although Siger had already departed with his uncle.

Outside in the four-wheeler, Holmes shook his head. "I had forgotten how sensitive and proud Wesley can sometimes be," he stated. "He and I were always competitors as boys. I think that he was rather gratified when he learned that I did not finish my degrees at either Oxford or Cambridge, while he went on to become a doctor. Upon the completion of his medical degree, he returned here and has become an important man in the area. It cannot sit well for him to have me return and intrude on what he thinks of as his own personal bailiwick."

Tenley asked where Holmes wished to go next. "To visit my brother, Sherrinford," replied Holmes.

PART IV: THE PRISONER

It was only a matter of minutes to wind through the village to an odd building, standing alone from its neighbors and quite tall for the area, reaching three stories above the ground. On the top floor I could see barred windows.

"This is new," said Holmes, looking at the building.

"Yes sir," said Tenley. "It was constructed a year or so ago. A man in York, Sir Clive Owenby, put up the money. He made some talk about providing proper facilities for the local law enforcement authorities. I believe that he is a close acquaintance of your brother Mycroft."

We entered the building and began to divest ourselves of our wet outer garments. From a side office emerged a short, powerfully built man in a spotless uniform. I was not surprised when he introduced himself as Constable Worth.

"It is a pleasure to meet you, gentlemen," he said, shaking our hands. "Unpleasant business all around, I'm afraid."

117

"Have you learned anything further since we last spoke?" asked Tenley, cutting through the introductions.

"Not a thing, sir. The prisoner has not made any further statements."

"I meant from anyone else, such as members of Wilkies's campsite."

"No, sir. Haven't been back out there."

Tenley gestured to us. "These men will be going up to visit Mr. Holmes. May I have the key to the cell?"

Worth looked surprised. "Sir, these cells are my responsibility . . . ."

"The keys, Constable," said Tenley, holding out his hand. Worth reluctantly produced the keys, laying them in Tenley's palm.

Tenley immediately handed them to Holmes. "Top of the stairs, sir," he said. "I will stay down here with Constable Worth and discuss today's visit by Mr. Morland."

"But sir," said Worth. "The prisoner . . . These men are not authorized to just go up and open the door. They are members of his family, sir . . . . "

Tenley waved his hand. "These people are entirely trustworthy, and I vouch for them completely. Mr. Holmes and Dr. Watson have performed countless services for the government of this country. And young Siger, here, is training as well to continue his uncle's work."

Siger widened his eyes and pulled himself straighter, adding to the already existing impression of great height and leanness. Holmes caught my eye, his lips turned up in a minuscule smile. As one, we turned from Tenley and Worth.

We started upstairs, leaving Worth looking uncomfortable in the feeble light of the entrance hall. We reached a landing on the stairs, and then climbed to the first floor, which seemed to consist of a series of closed rooms all opening from the small landing by the stairs. Only a single gaslight burned on that floor to illuminate our progress. We turned toward the next set of stairs, moving past the final landing before reaching the top

118

floor. I arrived first, and waited for my friends, all of whom were more out of breath than I.

Holmes stepped in front of me to a closed door. Turning the knob revealed a short hallway, with metal-barred cells on each side. The room was lit by a single lamp hanging in the hall from the ceiling between the cells. Siger stepped through the door and stopped at the first cell on the left. Taking the keys from Holmes, he opened the door.

A man was sitting in the shadows at the back of the cell. He stirred, rose, and stepped forward into the light. He was several inches over six feet, and looked much like his brothers, but mostly like his son William.

He thrust his arms out when he saw Sherlock Holmes and smiled. The expression lit his face with kindness and good-hearted joy, and in spite of the grimness of the location, with the rain pounding on the roof above us, I grinned myself.

Sherrinford Holmes hugged his younger brother and laughed. I glanced at Siger and William and saw that they were smiling as well. I knew immediately that Sherrinford was a good man, and could not be in any way responsible for that of which he was accused. There was an air of kindness about him that was I unable to define, but it existed nonetheless. It was as if someone had managed to combine Sherlock Holmes and Father Christmas.

I missed whatever Sherrinford mumbled to Holmes. Then he released his brother and reached for his sons, who also received great hugs. Then he turned to me. I feared that I would be clasped to the big man, but instead he thrust out a great paw of a hand and grasped mine, shaking it and introducing himself.

"I am so sorry it has taken us so long to meet, Dr. Watson," he cried. "It is as much my fault as my brother's, I'm afraid. I'll wager he never even told you that he had people up here in Yorkshire, did he?" Without waiting for an answer, he continued. "It has always been his way. However, I have not made my way down to London to see him, either. Not in all the years that he has been down there. Unforgivable, doctor, simply unforgivable on my part."

119

He stepped back, and looked at Holmes in mock sternness. "I understand that Dr. Watson was wounded in Afghanistan, Sherlock, shortly before the two of you met." Holmes nodded, and Sherrinford continued. "I now perceive that the wound was in his leg. Tell me, why on earth did you make him take the room upstairs from your sitting room at your lodgings? Shouldn't you have offered to let the wounded war veteran have the more easily accessible bedroom on the first floor near the sitting room, while you took the one upstairs on the second?"

He moved back into the cell, gesturing for us to enter. I had known Sherlock Holmes at that time for over fifteen years, counting the years when he had disappeared. I had seen his brother, Mycroft, on numerous occasions since meeting him in the fall of 1888. By now I should have been used to the deductions of the Holmes brothers, and if I could not immediately follow their logic to understand how their conclusions were reached, I should have at least learned to keep my mouth shut. However, as was usually the case, I had to know.

"How did you know that my bedroom is upstairs and your brother's bedroom on the first floor?" I asked.

Sherrinford smiled. "Siger?" he asked, "will you explain it to the doctor?"

Siger stepped forward, his hands clasped in front of him, as if he were reciting his multiplication tables at school. "Was it Dr. Watson's breathing?" he asked.

Sherrinford nodded. "Exactly. Go ahead."

Holmes moved into the cell, leaning against one of the walls. Sherrinford gestured toward his cot, offering me a place to sit. I shook my head, and Sherrinford seated himself in the middle of the rickety structure.

Siger took a deep breath. "When we reached this floor, Dr. Watson arrived first, while Uncle Sherlock, William, and I arrived seconds later. No doubt you had been expecting us, and you were listening for our footsteps. You heard Dr. Watson first, during the several seconds he was alone at the top of the steps, and you realized from his limp who he was. You also could tell that he was not out of breath. Then you heard the rest of us arrive, and we paused to catch our wind for a few seconds, before entering the cells.

"You already knew about Dr. Watson's war service from his narrative, *A Study In Scarlet*, as well as other published accounts. You were able to determine that his wound was in the leg, both from the limp, and also from the fact that he is quite comfortable with it at this point, sixteen years later, so much so that he was able to climb the steps better than his companions.

"The evenness of the doctor's breathing indicated that he is used to climbing to the second floor on a regular basis, while Uncle Sherlock is not. Obviously both men are conditioned to climb to the first floor, where their sitting room is located, but since Uncle Sherlock has not had to get used to climbing any higher on a regular basis, his bedroom is obviously on the same floor as the sitting room at their lodgings, while the doctor's room is one floor higher."

"Absolutely right," said Sherrinford. "And of course, Siger, as active as you are, there are not many steps for you to climb at our house, either, so you were as out of breath as your uncle."

"But why couldn't I be used to climbing to the second story somewhere else," I asked. "Why do you assume I have only conditioned myself to climb that many steps to my rooms at our lodgings? Couldn't I have done so at my practice, or at a hospital?"

"I knew from Sherlock's letters that you had sold your practice and had placed your self back in harness with my brother," stated Sherrinford. "It seemed logical that the only place you were regularly climbing that many stairs would be at your home." He looked at Holmes. "However, Sherlock, you didn't answer my question. Why did you make Dr. Watson take the higher room all those years ago when he was a recently invalided soldier?"

Holmes looked slightly uncomfortable, and even, perhaps, guilty. "When I found the rooms in Baker Street, I knew that I could not afford them by myself. When I mentioned the need to find a fellow lodger to my friend Stamford, at Bart's, I did not seriously believe that anything would come of it, and I never really thought that I would be able to obtain the rooms. When Stamford introduced me to Watson, I immediately saw that he had been wounded in Afghanistan, but in all honesty, it simply never occurred to me to offer him the bedroom adjacent to the sitting room on the first floor.

"I suppose that I rationalized that since I had been the one to find the rooms I should take the more accessible one. Also, to be honest, I was not certain that Watson would be residing there for any length of time"

He smiled in my direction. "I believed that a combination of my increased professional success, allowing me to afford the rooms by myself, as well as my generally poor attractiveness as a fellow lodger, would soon encourage you to move on to something better. And I must admit, that until now, I have selfishly never thought of the added discomfort climbing those extra steps must have caused you, my dear Watson."

Holmes lifted his hand. "It is far too late to ask, but would you like to trade rooms?"

I laughed, and everyone joined in. "Of course not," I said. "Climbing up and down those steps was probably excellent therapy for me. Besides," I added, "I was so lazy in those early days that climbing to my room every time you needed the sitting room to meet with one of your clients was the only exercise I took."

Sherrinford nodded. "Excellent job of reasoning, Siger," he said to his son.

Siger looked surprised. "But I was just explaining what *you* had determined," he said.

Sherrinford waved this away, and turned to Holmes. "I don't have to reason anything out to determine why you are here," he said. "Roberta must have contacted you."

"Actually, she contacted Mycroft, who in turn enlisted the efforts of Inspector Tenley, followed by Watson and myself."

Sherrinford nodded. "What do you need to ask me?"

"Simply begin at the beginning, and I will ask questions as needed."

"Well," said Sherrinford, rubbing his hands together and settling on the cot, "about two weeks ago, in the morning, a group of wagons arrived at the farm. The lead wagon pulled a little closer to the house, and a man hopped down. I was in the barn and went out to meet him.

"Of course, it was Wilkies. He introduced himself, and pointed to his daughter, who had remained on the seat of the wagon. He said that he and his group were heading into the north for the summer, and they wondered if they could stop on our land for a week or so before moving on. They seemed respectable enough, and I agreed. I directed them to the southern fields, where I knew the conditions would be pleasant, with shade trees, and there would be plenty of water from the stream.

"That night, after they had set up camp, I walked over to see how they were doing. Wilkies invited me into his tent, a large, spacious affair that was obviously military surplus. There were nearly a dozen other tents, spread around a central area, and each with its own campfire. A rope paddock had been set up somewhat downstream for the livestock.

"Wilkies instructed his daughter to prepare tea. She did so without comment, moving silently about the tent, and, if I may speculate, somewhat resentfully of my presence. While she worked, I questioned Wilkies about the nature of his group. His description led me to believe that they are some sort of offshoot of Druidism, with an eccentric mixture of Christianity, Egyptian pantheism, and some Germanic mythology as well. He had apparently been a Church of England theology student in his early twenties, before developing his own unique beliefs. He published some tracts ten or fifteen years ago explaining his theology, and at one point had started his own church, where he attracted a few loyal followers. At some time, he was forced to leave his church building, and he and his congregation took to the road, traveling throughout the countryside, much like gypsies from north to south, and back again.

"I visited his tent every two or three days, questioning him about his beliefs. In the second week, I was becoming somewhat curious as to when he intended to depart, as his people had shown no signs of preparing to leave. However, I never came right out and asked him, and he never volunteered the information on his own.

"The night of the murder was simply another visit, and there was no anger between us. In fact, there was not much conversation at all. He and I sat on camp stools in front of his tent, facing the fire, in companionable silence. I saw no signs of his daughter, Sophia, although it is possible she may have been in the tent. As to what she claims to have heard, I can only say that if she believes that conversation to have taken place between me and her father, she is completely mistaken. Perhaps she heard him arguing later, with someone else. I do not know what the phrase 'the true path,' which was attributed to me, refers to."

"Did you ever have any conversations with any of the other followers, either at the camp or elsewhere?" Holmes asked.

"Never," replied his brother. "As far as I know, none of them ever ventured away from camp, and they kept to themselves when I was there. For that matter, Sophia never spoke to me either. She would simply meet my eyes with a somewhat reserved expression before looking away, or gesturing me toward the tent where her father and I would talk."

Holmes was silent for several minutes, before asking, "What can you tell me of Augustus Morland?"

Sherrinford cleared his throat and looked at Siger. "Have you been telling Sherlock of your suspicions of Morland?"

"He came to the house today," said Siger. "He claimed that he wanted to offer his help, after he had been told of your arrest by Constable Worth." Then he added, "How did you know of my suspicions about him?"

Sherrinford waved a hand. "Fathers know everything, son." He turned back to his brother. "I have met Morland half-a-dozen times or so in the last few months. He has been trying to buy up all the land in this area, including ours." He went on to relate the same narrative of events that had earlier been provided to us by Roberta. "He appears to be trying to create an unbroken estate stretching from here all the way to the sea. And he seems to have the money and resources to do so, eventually. If he doesn't get our land, he will simply buy some around it until he gets the contiguous layout that he desires."

Holmes shifted away from the wall. "Have you conferred with legal counsel?"

"Not yet," replied Sherrinford. "I believe that Worth has forgotten about it. Tenley and I talked earlier today, and we both felt that at this point it was not necessary. I am willing to wait here for a little while longer while the investigation progresses. Hopefully, this will lull the real murderer into a false sense of security, if he believes that his plan to frame me has been completely accepted." Sherrinford stood. "Can I tell you anything else?"

"I think that I have heard enough for tonight," he said. "Is there anything we can do for you? Can we bring you anything?"

"No, no, I am quite all right," Sherrinford replied. "Worth is basically a good fellow, for all his pretensions. I am quite sure that you will have me out of here in a day or so."

"I am confident of that as well," said Holmes. "I begin to see where to pull the red thread running through this tangled skein."

Sherrinford stepped forward, and Holmes shook his hand. Then Sherrinford shook mine as well, before drawing his sons into another hug. "Give my love to your mother," he said.

"We will," replied Siger, quietly. We left the cell, and Siger solemnly relocked the door.

Downstairs, he handed the keys to Tenley, who was standing near the front door. In a side room we could see Worth, sitting at his desk, looking chastened and somewhat embarrassed. I nodded to the man, and we left the building. Tenley followed in a moment, after returning the keys to Worth.

In the four-wheeler, Tenley said, "What next, gentlemen?"

"I need to send some wires, and then back to the farm for the night, I suppose," replied Holmes. The ever-patient Griffin turned the horse, and then drove the four-wheeler for a few short minutes to the office where Holmes jumped down, going in to send his telegrams. Siger, William, Tenley, and I waited in the four-wheeler, grateful that the rain had stopped, although a cold damp wind still blew.

Holmes returned in a minute, climbed in, and we set off for the Holmes farm. It was not long before we arrived. Tenley asked, "What do you have planned for tomorrow, Mr. Holmes?"

"If you and Griffin could be back here by about nine o'clock, I believe that we will interview Miss Sophia at the campsite."

"Very good," said Tenley, as we climbed down. "See you in the morning, then."

As they drove away, the door opened, spilling light into the damp yard. We went inside to find that Roberta had prepared something of a feast. Siger passed on the good wishes of his father, and we sat down to eat. Over the years I had often thought of Sherlock Holmes as a lonely man, buried in his studies and thoughts. That night, I was able to see a new side of him, as part of a family that treasured and cherished him. As Holmes's friend, I was given some of that affection as well. The entire evening was somewhat muted, due to the absence of Sherrinford and the awful events that had led to his arrest. However, in spite of that, there was an optimism that the incarceration was only temporary, and the warm feelings of that house could not be quelled.

As we climbed the stairs to our rooms later that night, I told Holmes, "I am honored to meet your family. They are fine people, indeed."

"Yes, they are," he replied. "I must never take them for granted. Perhaps I should try to visit here more often."

"I agree, Holmes. I heartily agree." We reached the door of my room.

"Good night, Holmes."

He continued down the hallway. Over his shoulder, he said "And good night to you as well, Watson."

PART V: THE CAMP

We arose early next morning to find that Roberta had prepared a large farm breakfast, which I greeted with enthusiasm. I was unsurprised to see that Holmes picked at his food, and seemed content to consume several cups of strong

126

black coffee. William kept pace with my appetite, but Siger seemed to eat even less than his uncle. He looked tired, and acted rather nervous, glancing at Holmes often before directing his eyes elsewhere around the room.

After William and I had eaten as much as we could, William pushed back from the table and stood, announcing that he wished us good luck, and that he would like to accompany us but someone must continue to direct the daily activities of the farm. With a wave he departed. Siger, who had grown more and more nervous, finally blurted out,

"Uncle, may I have a word with you and Dr. Watson? Outside," he added, cutting his eyes toward his mother. Roberta smiled, but did not say anything. Thanking her for a wonderful meal, we stepped out of the house and into the yard. Siger was carrying a worn knapsack, which he had kept beside him throughout breakfast.

Holmes pulled out his watch. "Tenley should be here in ten minutes or so. What is it, Siger?"

His nephew appeared uncertain, now that he had his uncle's attention. After a few awkward seconds of silence, he said, "I have discovered something important, uncle, but in doing so I may have jeopardized your case."

Holmes indicated that he should continue. "Last night," said Siger, "I could not sleep. Without taking time to explain all my reasoning and the various dead ends I let my mind travel, I finally came to the conclusion that Mr. Morland must somehow be involved in this matter. So I arose and slipped out of the house. I then made my way over the fields to Morland's."

Holmes looked quickly at me, and then back to his nephew. A glint had caught fire in Holmes's hooded eyes. "And what did you find?" he asked.

"What I expected to find," Siger said, opening the knapsack. "And more that I did not expect." He reached in, and pulled out a rolled bundle of white bloodstained cloth. Glancing toward the house to make sure he was unobserved, Siger dropped the knapsack and began to unroll his discovery. His hands revealed some sort of religious robe, almost completely soaked in dried

127

blood. As the bundle was nearly unrolled, he stopped and carefully extricated two items which had been tucked in the center.

The first was a dagger, its thin narrow blade about six inches long. It seemed quite old, and the handle appeared to be made of iron, with blunt and clumsy runes engraved in it. The blade was covered with dried blood. The second item from the bundle was something far more sinister.

I had seen a thing like it once before, years earlier, although I never expected see one again, and surely not in the heart of beautiful Yorkshire. It was a Hand of Glory, the foul device used by witches' covens while practicing their hated black magic. In the early eighties, Holmes and I had been involved in the destruction of a nest of the evil practitioners. At the time, I had been shocked to my core by the evil to which the human heart was capable of sinking, in spite of my experiences on many continents and the horrors I had seen in war.

I must have gasped, because both Holmes and Siger looked away from the bundle and toward me. I swallowed and said, "Holmes, what can it mean?"

He did not reply. Instead, he reached for the white robe. Taking it from Siger, he finished unfolding it. He searched for a moment with his long thin fingers before finding what he sought. On the back of the robe, centered in the place equivalent to where Wilkies's fatal wound had been on his body, was a long ragged slit. This part of the robe was the most blood-soaked portion of the whole garment.

"This is what Wilkies was wearing when he was murdered," said Holmes, pushing his finger through the hole. "It is some sort of ceremonial robe. For some reason, he was changed into conventional clothing after death." He rotated the robe to examine the clean neck line. "And his throat was not slit while he was wearing this. As we believed, it took place post-mortem."

He then held up the knife, turning it from side to side in the morning sunlight. "I think it is safe to say that this is the murder weapon," he said. "The width of the blade corresponds to some of the marks on the body." Turning to Siger, he asked, "Where did you find this?"

"It was in one of Morland's stable buildings, an unused one, in an empty stall under some straw."

"How did you know to look there?"

"It wasn't the first place that I looked," replied Siger. "Of course, I couldn't get in the house, but I did think that I would be able to search most of the out-buildings."

"Weren't you afraid of being caught?" I asked.

Siger replied, with a look that must have made his uncle proud, "When I search, I do not get caught."

"Why did you decide to search Morland's premises?" asked Holmes.

"I simply reasoned that he, of all the people currently around here, would have the most reason to frame my father, simply because Father will not sell him our farm. If someone in the religious camp wanted to murder Wilkies, they would have done so without involving my father."

"That is not necessarily so," said Holmes, "but no matter, right now. Did you expect to find this?" he asked, holding up the robe and the items that had been hidden within it.

"Not exactly," said Siger. "I knew that Wilkies had not been murdered in the clothing in which he was found. I decided to look for the actual murder clothing, which must have been taken away by the murderer. If my assumption was correct, and Morland was involved, then logically he would have taken the clothing.

"Of course, there was every reason to think that it could have been already destroyed, or hidden somewhere in the fields, or even buried or burned. However, if I spent the night exploring Mr. Morland's barns, all I could lose would be a night's sleep, and look what I found." He gestured at the robe, and added, "Of course, I did not expect to find this, exactly. I thought I would possibly just discover another suit similar to the one that Wilkies was wearing when his body was found."

Holmes was silent for a moment, and then he began to re-roll the bundle, making sure that the dagger and the Hand of Glory were concealed within. "It is very important," he said, "when gathering information in a criminal case, to protect the chain of evidence. By that, I mean that one must be able to demonstrate in a court of law that the evidence has been untainted and unaltered before it is discovered by a legitimate and verifiable source." He pushed the bundle into Siger's knapsack. "I realize that you took this in order to show it to me, and also to make sure that it was not removed and destroyed in the meantime. However, the authenticity of the evidence is now somewhat compromised."

Siger lowered his head. "I am sorry, uncle."

"I agree with you that somehow, Morland is involved in this matter. I had decided that yesterday, before your important discovery. However, if the matter came to court as it stands now, Morland's attorneys could argue that he was an innocent victim of a plot, or that one of his own employees had hidden the items without his knowledge. In fact, they could even argue that you, Siger, had been involved in the murder yourself and that you had pretended to find the items at Morland's farm in order to frame *him*."

Siger looked up with an apprehensive expression. "Inspector Tenley would tell you the same thing," continued Holmes. "By removing this evidence, its effectiveness is decreased or eliminated altogether." Holmes handed the knapsack to Siger, who widened his eyes in surprise. "Inspector Tenley would tell you that, I suppose, if he knew about it."

Holmes turned and glanced down the lane, toward the approaching four-wheeler containing Tenley and Griffin. "We are going to Morland's house later this morning," said Holmes. "Would you be so kind, Siger, to slip away from us at some point so that you can replace the items in question where you found them? Without being observed, of course. We are taking a chance that they will not be destroyed in the meantime, until we are ready to find them legitimately. Also, we can only hope that their absence has not already been discovered, causing the murderer to move before we are ready to outflank him."

Holmes continued to stare at the approaching vehicle, while Siger shouldered the knapsack. He turned to me with a relieved smile on his face. I reached out and gripped his shoulder.

The four-wheeler had barely stopped before Tenley jumped down, reaching us in a few steps. "These arrived this morning, Mr. Holmes, from Mycroft," he said, holding a stack of telegrams out in front of him.

"They were addressed to both of us, so I've already read them. I think you will find them interesting."

Holmes took the forms and quickly studied them, one after another, before passing them to me. As I finished them, I handed them on to Siger.

"Will we be going to Mr. Morland's, then?" asked Tenley.

"Not yet," replied Holmes. "First I want to go to Wilkies's camp, and to meet his daughter."

In the four-wheeler, I pondered the astounding information I had read in the long telegraph forms. Obviously Mycroft, working for the government, had no hesitation at sending extensively long wires when the mood suited him.

The telegram forms consisted of one long message, relating the curious and sinister history of Augustus Morland. It seemed that Morland had moved to Yorkshire from Manchester, as we had already heard. However, his background was slightly more convoluted than the story of his origin in Manchester had led us to believe. He had graduated from university nearly twenty-five years earlier, and had immediately left on a year-long tour of the continent. While this was not unusual, the subsequent events were. Soon after his arrival in one of the smaller German spa towns, he had disappeared. The local police were unable to find him, and for over a year there was no sign of him whatsoever. During that time, his mother in Manchester had sickened with despair and died.

At that time, in the early 1870's, Germany had still been a patchwork of small kingdoms, duchies, and petty fiefdoms, with little cooperation or communication between them. It had proved nearly impossible to discover anything about the disappearance and whereabouts of young Morland. Then, over a year after he had gone missing, Morland had resurfaced, claiming that he had been kidnapped by anarchists who had argued amongst themselves the entire time about whether to kill him outright or request a ransom. Finally he had managed to escape and make his way to safety. However, he had refused to return home to England, instead stating that he preferred to remain in Germany.

His father had begged him to come home, sending urgent letters and telegrams, but young Morland refused. The father, already sickened by the death of his wife and the extended mystery of his missing son, was too weak to travel to Germany in order to try in person to convince the young man that he should return to England. The father soon died, and Morland inherited the estates.

Morland remained ensconced in Germany for nearly a quarter of a century, maintaining his business interests from there, and increasing his wealth many times over. It was only in the last year or so that he had returned to his family home in Manchester, where he had lived for a few months before moving again, this time to Yorkshire, where he began his bullying acquisitions of the surrounding farm lands.

The final sheets of the telegram revealed that Mycroft Holmes, as well as his nephew Bancroft, had become interested in Morland several months earlier. A closer investigation was made into the man's past, and Mycroft's agents had recently determined that the man was not actually Morland at all, but rather an imposter who had been set in place years earlier, following the original abduction and murder of the actual young man.

"I knew it!" stated Siger, as we discussed the matter in the rocking four-wheeler. "I knew that there was something wrong about the man."

"Is the telegraph agent who took this information completely reliable?" Holmes asked Tenley. "Can he keep the information confidential?"

"He is one of my men," Tenley replied. "He can be trusted."

Holmes eyed Tenley speculatively. "You do not seem surprised by what is in these messages," he said.

"Your brother, Mycroft, keeps a pretty close eye on things," he said. "Especially around here. Apparently, when Morland started buying up vast amounts of land, it came to Mycroft's attention pretty quickly."

"I would wager that you knew about it as well," said Holmes. "Probably for quite a while before this murder actually took place." He shifted in his seat. "Why wasn't I told about this aspect of the case to begin with?"

"Your brother felt that you would benefit by beginning your investigation with an open mind. He was not necessarily convinced that Morland's background and activities were directly related to the murder. Mycroft decided to reveal Morland's background to you after you had gotten the initial lay of the land. At that point, you could determine Morland's relevance to the investigation. However, your wires to London last night indicated that you had already decided that Morland is somehow involved."

Holmes asked, "Are you actually an inspector with the Yard, or do your responsibilities require you to pursue different activities?"

Tenley smiled. "They know me at the Yard. However, much of my work is carried out more in your brother's purview."

"I thought as much," Holmes said, nodding. "You are one of my brother's agents." Holmes folded the telegraph forms and put them in his pocket. "Were you assigned to this area as part of your responsibilities to my brother's department?"

Tenley nodded. "Keeping an eye on Morland is just part of my job up here."

Holmes gestured around him. "Just how much land has this German agent actually bought?"

"Enough," Tenley replied. "Too much. We think that he hopes to obtain even more, so that he can create some sort of vast staging area, with buffer zones on either side so that no one will be able to notice or tell."

"Tell what?" asked Siger. "That there are German soldiers surreptitiously landing in England?"

"Soldiers?" I asked. "Is it to be war, then?"

133

"Eventually," said Tenley, without emotion. "Not this year, maybe not through the rest of this century, or even into the first part of the next, but it is coming. The Kaiser is interested in creating his own global empire, and he is too resentful of the British Empire, as well as the restraining influence of his grandmother, Queen Victoria. Eventually the Germans will lash out."

"Mycroft and I have been predicting as much for years," said Holmes. "However, as respected as Mycroft is, he has had the devil of a time convincing his superiors of the obvious facts."

" 'A prophet hath no honor in his own country.' Eh, Mr. Holmes?" asked Tenley with a smile.

"John 4:44," replied both Holmes and Siger at the same time. They looked at each other with surprise, and then they began to laugh. Tenley and I joined in. Griffin, as emotionless as ever, continued to guide the horses. We were soon within sight of Wilkies's camp.

As we had been told the day before, the campsite consisted of a loose grouping of tents. These were clustered underneath the trees that grew beside the stream watering the south side of the Holmes land. From my military days, I was able to quickly confirm that the tents were military castoffs of a style that had gone out of date at least twenty years before.

Each of the tents was a dull brown color, the original dyes having long been faded and replaced by weathering and mildew of too many years of use. Each tent's ugly hue, however, was tempered somewhat by the canvas patches of varying shades that were randomly sewn along their sides, giving them something of a gypsy air.

Tenley led us to the larger and more central tent, in front of which sat a young woman on a camp stool. Before her were the smoking remains of a fire, apparently left to die following the completion of her breakfast preparations. As we approached, the woman stood to face us, dropping her arms and holding her fisted hands at her sides.

"Sophia," said Tenley, "these are the men from London who are here to investigate your father's death. This is Mr. Sherlock

134

Holmes, and Dr. Watson. And this young man is Siger Holmes, the son of Sherrinford Holmes."

"The son of a murderer, you mean!" she hissed, turning quickly in Siger's direction. He was surprised, and took a startled step backward before remembering himself and holding his ground.

Sophie Wilkies was a sallow young woman in her early twenties, not much over five feet in height. Her hair was loose, with shading somewhere between black and dark brown. Her hair was actually her most attractive feature, and it shone in the morning sunlight, obviously freshly brushed. She was somewhat unfortunate in her facial features, as she had bushy eyebrows similar to her late father's, on a prominent ridge shading her dark eyes. Also, her lower lip was heavy and pendulous, and tended to sag toward her rather weak chin, revealing white but quite crooked lower teeth. When she spoke, her lip would tighten, giving her whole face a look of determination, As she completed her thought, however, her face would relax and her lip would droop back down, again revealing her unfortunate and rather distracting mouth.

"Miss Wilkies," said Holmes, "I was wondering whether you could repeat for us the conversation that you said that you heard the night your father was murdered."

"I didn't *say* I heard it. I *did* hear it! That man had come around here again, that *murderer*, and started in browbeating my father about how he had abandoned 'the true path,' whatever that means. They had discussed it every single night that the man visited, but the night when he killed my father, he was much more angry about it. He even threatened my father. He said that anyone who turned away from the 'true path' would not have long in this world to reconsider his mistake."

"You say he threatened your father?" asked Tenley. "You did not mention that when we spoke of this matter before."

"I just remembered it," said the girl, crossing her arms defiantly.

"What is the 'true path'?" asked Holmes.

"I do not know," said the girl. "My father has been the shepherd of this flock since before I was born. When I was a little girl, we had a church building, but my father decided that his calling was to lead the faithful to sojourn at the holy sites of Britain, reawakening the lost beliefs. In the last few years, we have occasionally traveled to the continent as well, visiting holy sites in France, Germany, and even Belgium."

"How does your congregation finance itself?" asked Holmes. I had wondered the same thing myself. The condition of the campsite did not indicate that funds were immediately available for pilgrimages across the Channel.

"My father inherited some money as a young man," Sophia answered. "And members of our congregation have funds of their own that they provide for us all when they join our group. They contribute as needed. As you can see, our wants are simple." She gestured toward the other tents, where several members of the group were going about their own business, mending clothing, or tending to pots suspended over small fires.

"Who will lead your group, now that your father is gone?" I asked.

"I will," the girl said simply. "My father would have wanted it that way."

"Did your father have any enemies?" asked Holmes.

"I see what you are doing!" cried the girl. "You want me to say that maybe someone else could have killed my father. Well, no one else did. It was this boy's father who did it! I will swear to it!"

Holmes and Tenley continued to ask questions for a few more minutes, but the girl provided no additional information, and could not be swayed in her single-minded belief that the murderer of her father was Sherrinford Holmes. Her dogmatic assertions tended to reveal her somewhat limited intellectual gifts. Siger stood to the side, watching uncomfortably as the girl's story remained unshaken. His knuckles, gripping the straps of his knapsack, were white.

Finally we thanked the girl and left. She flounced into her tent and pulled the flap down, shutting herself inside. We started to walk toward the four-wheeler, where patient Griffin sat hunched in the warming morning sunshine. We were thirty or forty feet from the girl's tent when an old man, sitting on a stool in front of a much smaller tent, hailed us.

"Her father never talked any about 'the true path' with anyone," he said. "The only people who ever discussed that around here was Sophia herself, and that rich man who has been coming around here to see her."

We crowded closer, keeping our voices low so that no one would overhear us. "What rich man?" Holmes asked.

"That Morland fellow," the old man replied. "He has been here several times since we made camp. He and Sophia huddle and whisper to each other, usually near my tent. They don't pay me any attention, and they don't seem to mind talking in front of me."

"What have they said?" asked Tenley.

"Sophia talks about how she is the one that's going to lead everyone back to the 'true path,' and that what her father has always believed is simply a weak and watered-down reflection of the truth. Morland whispers to her, telling her how right she is, dear, and they will lead the people together, dear. It right makes me sick."

"What is the 'true path,' then?" asked Holmes.

"I don't really know," said the old man. "From what I could hear, Sophia believes that her father was right to visit the old places, the great stones and ruins and such, but that when we were there, he was wasting his time trying to get in touch with the wrong kind of spirits. It sounds to me as if the spirits Sophia wants to reach are quite a bit more grim than what her father believed in."

"And what exactly did her father believe in?"

"Well, I don't know exactly," said the old man.

"What?" I said, reflecting the astonishment of my friends.

"Well, I don't. I don't believe in all this stuff. Don't pay any attention to it, really. My wife did, though, and when she wanted to travel with these people, I didn't really object to it. I had roamed some in my younger days, and always found it agreeable. When my wife wanted to go a-traveling I didn't mind at all, even though it meant going about with these folks, but I never was really a part of this group. I just enjoyed the journey, you see, and got to visit some places I might not have seen otherwise.

"I had inherited a little money, and once long ago I had a store that I later sold for enough of a profit to pay for my daily bread, so I can afford to play at this game with these people. They all seem nice enough, and harmless, too, I suppose. All except for Sophia. After my wife died a year or so ago, I decided to just keep going about with them. No one has said anything against it, and I guess I've been a part of the group for so long that no one questions it anymore, even though my wife was the real believer."

"How often has Mr. Morland been here?" asked Holmes.

"Usually every day, since we started camping here a couple of weeks ago. At first he spoke to both Wilkies and Sophia, but later he just came by to see Sophia by herself. I don't even know if her father realized it, because he was usually in his tent at the time, praying, or taking a nap."

The old man shifted in his seat and leaned forward, lowering his voice somewhat. "Morland hasn't been back here since Wilkies was murdered, though." He glanced at Sophia's tent. "I'll tell you something else, as well. This wasn't the first time we had met this Mr. Morland. He first showed up a couple of years ago, when we were traveling through Germany. He looked a lot different then, wasn't dressed nearly so fine, but it was him.

"Depending on where we camp, we sometimes get visitors from the nearby towns who are curious about whatever it is that Wilkies was teaching. In some German town, I forget which, Morland showed up one day with a group of those people. It wasn't long before he and Sophia met each other. Even then, the two of them would find time to walk apart from everyone else and whisper to one another. I first thought it was something romantic, but all Sophia seems to be interested in is reforming her father's religion, and Morland seems happy to encourage it."

138

"You said he looked different," asked Holmes. "In what way?"

"He looked more . . . German when we met him in Germany," replied the old man. "His beard and mustache were cut in a different way, and he walked stiffer, somehow. He didn't wear fancy clothes like he does now, but what he did wear still seemed . . . expensive, if you know what I mean. And of course he spoke German. Sophia speaks some German too, you know, although they've been speaking in English whenever Morland visits this camp. I heard that Sophia's mother was originally from Germany. Maybe that's how she learned it."

Despite further questioning, the old man could provide no additional information, and he assured us that he would not be telling anyone else about our conversation, especially Sophia. We thanked him, and Holmes stated that he appreciated the old man's observations. "That's *my* religion," the fellow replied. "Watching people. There isn't any better entertainment than to sit back, smoke a pipe or two, and watch folks going about their daily business. Sometimes it gets a little tedious, I will admit, but generally after a while someone will do something worth watching."

We stepped away from him, to the center of the camp, and Holmes thought for a moment. Then he led us closer to Sophia's tent, while telling me, "Watson, I need you to feign an illness. Just for a moment or two, that's a good chap."

Without giving me time to protest or prepare myself, he signaled that I was to begin. I froze for just a moment, before letting out a feeble moan. Holmes's brows contracted in irritation, and I could tell that he expected a better effort from me. With a sigh, I began to stagger while braying like some farm animal that has gotten into fermented feed. As I began to sag, lowering myself to a less dusty part of the clearing, I could see that Holmes was running to Sophia's tent, calling her forth for help.

In a moment, Sophia was kneeling beside me as I groaned and attempted to keep her attention. Over her shoulder, I could see other members of the community gathering around us while

Holmes slipped unseen into Sophia's tent. Sophia kept asking me where it was hurting and what the matter was, but I pretended not to understand her, repeating this process until I saw Holmes exiting the tent and walking toward us.

Holmes nodded, and my illness miraculously healed itself. Within moments I was able to rise to my feet, thanking Sophia for her help, and assuring her that I had simply had an attack related to a fever picked up during my war service overseas, and that there was no need to be concerned. She seemed puzzled, but then with a gesture that she was washing her hands of me, she turned and went back into her tent.

As we walked to four-wheeler, Holmes said, "Excellent, Watson. I almost believed it myself."

"I hope you got what you came for," I whispered with irritation.

"What were you looking for?" asked Siger as our four-wheeler rolled away from the camp.

"This," replied Holmes, fishing a pair of folded notes from his waistcoat pocket. "Finding them was a long shot, but it will save us some trouble, I think."

He handed the papers to Siger, who unfolded them and spread them on his knee, where Tenley and I could see them. The first was simply a scrap of paper with a supply list scribbled on it. It was on poor quality paper, and the handwriting was poorly formed and uneducated. "That is a sample of Sophia's handwriting," said Holmes. "I thought it might come in handy later for a little idea that I have."

The second sheet of paper was about five inches square, and of exceptional thickness and good quality. The top edge was somewhat ragged, as if it had been torn, while the sides and bottom were straight and clean.

"It is a sheet of expensive stationery," said Holmes. "It was originally an inch or two longer."

"The portion with the monogram at the top has been torn off," said Siger, "in order to disguise the identity of the sender."

"It isn't disguised very well," said Tenley. "This paper is still somewhat unique. I'll bet we won't have to look too hard to find a matching sheet."

"Indeed," said Holmes. "That reminds me. Griffin, would you take us to Mr. Morland's house next, please?"

Griffin did not respond, but nudged his horses into a slightly faster gait.

"What do you make of the message?" asked Holmes.

It was handwritten, and quite short. In bold pen strokes, someone had written:

Nyy vf jryy. Frr lbh fbba. Z

"It is code," I said, causing everyone's eyes to raise and look toward me. Holmes's expression seemed somewhat irritated, while Siger and Tenley looked amused. I hastened to add, "Written by a man with a good quality pen and expensive black ink."

"Much better, Watson," said Holmes. "Does anyone want to take a try at decoding it?"

Tenley and I looked at one another, and then by tacit agreement, deferred to Siger, who was bent over the paper, his brows bunched in concentration.

"The letter *e* is the most common letter, and is likely to occur in double letters," he said softly. "However, there are several sets of double letters in this message, any of which could be *e*. If this were a simple substitution code . . . . "

He fell silent for a few moments, but his concentration never abated. The four-wheeler rocked down the road, and I glanced over at Holmes, who was looking fondly at his nephew. He turned his head to me, saw that I was watching him, and nodded in reply.

After a few moments, Siger's expression cleared, and he looked up with a joyous expression. "That wasn't so difficult," he said.

"It would have to be a simple code, so that Sophia could remember it," replied Holmes.

Tenley and I looked at one another, before I stated, "But what does it say?"

"Oh, that," said Siger. "It simply says '*All is well. See you soon. M.*'"

"M.," I said. "Morland!"

"Of course," said Holmes.

"Tell us about the code, Siger," said Tenley.

"Luckily, it was not too difficult," replied the young man. "The letter *e* is the most common letter used in the English language and can present itself as a double letter, such as in the word *seek*. This short message, however, had three sets of double letters, *yy*, which was used twice, *rr*, and *bb*. The simplest code is a substitution code, where one letter of the alphabet is substituted for another. If one wanted to make this code even simpler, the letters are not substituted at random, but are simply shifted, so that *a* can equal *b*, *b* equals *c*, and so on.

"Sometimes the coded alphabet will be reversed, so that *a* equals *z*, and *b* equals *y*. I quickly ran through a few of these combinations in my head, but none seemed to make sense. Then I thought that perhaps the coded alphabet had shifted more than just a letter or two. I started trying the message as if each double letter combination was *ee*. None of them worked until I tried *rr* as *ee*.

"This combination did produce an actual message, and I was able to see that the code simply shifted the alphabet so that *a* equaled *n*, *m* equaled *z*, and *n* equaled *a*. By shifting the alphabet exactly halfway, by thirteen of the twenty-six letters, perception of the more obvious substitutions would be avoided, but there was no need to have a key for the code lying around, which would have been the case if the letters were random substitutions.

"Excellent, Siger," said Tenley. "You have quite a gift for cryptography."

Siger looked somewhat bashful. "I simply read my Uncle Sherlock's monograph on the subject," he said, causing a momentary flash of pride of pass through Holmes's eyes. I was certain that he had already decoded the message before he ever revealed it to us. However, he had allowed his nephew the pleasure of solving the small mystery. I knew Sherlock Holmes was a wise man, but he continued to surprise me by revealing that wisdom in new and unexpected ways.

Griffin chose that moment to gesture ahead of us, muttering in his gruff and efficient manner, "Morland's."

It was time for the next act of our drama to begin.

PART VI: SETTING THE TRAP

We had been told by Roberta the day before that Augustus Morland was constructing a new, large home a few miles from where he currently lived. It seemed rather foolish to me, considering that the old manor house where he was currently living was very large on its own. I asked myself what use a single man could have for occupying such a large house while building an even bigger one. Then I remembered Tenley's description of a staging area, with hidden German troops quartered in secret until they could be turned loose on an unsuspecting nation.

Suddenly, the idea of huge houses standing throughout the largely empty Yorkshire countryside, each filled with smuggled arms and men over a long period of time and waiting until needed, made more sense.

We stopped at the front door and climbed down to the ground. There were several outbuildings scattered in the distance, but there did not seem to be any people working or carrying out the day-to-day tasks of running an estate. I wondered which of the buildings had been the location of Siger's grisly discovery.

As if reading my mind, Holmes said, "Siger, I would like for you to make a small reconnaissance of the outbuildings. See how many people are about. Afterwards, join us in the house, but as soon as it is convenient, try to wander off and obtain a sheet or two of Mr. Morland's stationery. You will know the type I mean. Some of it was used to write that coded message to Sophia."

Siger nodded and slipped away, as the rest of us turned to the front door, upon which Holmes knocked with authority. Tenley watched Siger disappear around the corner of the house in a speculative manner. In a moment, the door opened to reveal an old man, wearing ill-fitting and faded clothing. Holmes presented his card to the man. We were ushered in and asked to wait in the drawing room while the old fellow checked to see if Morland was available.

While Tenley perched himself in a chair, Holmes and I wandered about the room, looking at the artworks hanging from the walls and resting on table-tops. The items were obviously quite expensive, and showed good taste, but they were layered with accumulated dust. "These came with the house," said Holmes. "Morland cannot take credit for originally acquiring them."

Our inspection was interrupted by the arrival of Augustus Morland, who strode into the room looking somewhat peeved. However, he made an effort to sound gracious, welcoming us and offering us refreshments, which we refused. He motioned for us to be seated, then lowered himself into a chair with the window at his back, haloing his figure against the morning sun.

"What can I do for you gentlemen today?" he asked. I tried to perceive any hint of his hidden German ancestry, but he revealed no sign whatsoever, from his appearance to his perfect Manchester accent.

"We are simply speaking to some of the people in the area, and wanted to see if you had any relevant information to add to our investigation," said Holmes.

"Such as?" asked Morland, in his odd high-pitched voice.

"Oh, the usual type of thing. Are you aware of any problems Wilkies had with the neighbors? Have you heard of anyone speaking out against him, or possibly resenting that he and his congregation have been staying in the area?"

"No, no, nothing like that. In fact, I'm afraid the only stories I've heard about anyone having ill feelings toward Wilkies came from the testimony of his daughter, Sophia." He shook his head with a smile. "Such as it is."

Holmes raised an eyebrow. "What do you mean?"

"Oh, nothing, I suppose. From the few times I have seen her, she seems somewhat . . . limited in her thought processes. You may have met her yourself?" We nodded. "Then I think you must agree that she did not inherit her father's intellect."

"I had not heard it established that her father was an intellectual," said Holmes. "Am I to understand that you met him?"

"I visited their camp a few times, to introduce myself, and to see what type of people your brother was allowing to stay in our area."

"You were making rather free with Sherrinford Holmes's borders, weren't you, Mr. Morland?" asked Tenley. "After all, they were camped on his land. Wouldn't your visits be something of a trespass?"

"I, um, I didn't see it as a problem," said Morland. "We are all quite friendly here in the country. I meant no harm, I assure you. In any event, the important fact is that I was able to meet both Wilkies and his daughter, and it allowed me to form my opinions of Sophia, with which I'm sure you must agree. I would think that her limited intellectual powers would actually tend to support the veracity of her claim that your brother, Mr. Holmes, had serious words with Wilkies. Someone like Sophia, someone who is rather simple like that, would not be distracted by uncertainties. If she heard your brother arguing with Wilkies, and saying the things that he said to Wilkies, it would be definite."

"As you might imagine," replied Holmes, "my efforts are directed toward discovering a somewhat different interpretation of events."

"And Inspector Tenley here?" asked Morland. "Is he with you because he agrees that there is a different interpretation, or is it simply professional courtesy that causes him to accompany you? Do you believe, Inspector, that you have gotten the correct man in your cells?"

"I believe that based on the evidence initially presented, Constable Worth was correct in placing Mr. Sherrinford Holmes in custody," replied Tenley. "However, Mr. Sherlock Holmes here has a lot of clout, especially with my superiors, and it does not do any harm for me to accompany him during his further explorations of the case."

Morland nodded, then looked over us toward the entrance to the room. I turned to see Siger standing there, his knapsack held in front of him, looking much emptier than when we had arrived. I had not heard him come in. He nodded at his uncle, and then at Morland.

"Sorry, sir," he said, "I was just admiring your house a little bit."

Morland waved his hand. "Ah, boys must be boys. The temptation to explore is great, no doubt." He stood, as if indicating the interview was at an end. "But temptation must always be tempered with good manners, as well. Remember that, my boy."

Ringing for the servant, Morland said, "I'm sorry that I cannot help you in your quest to save your brother, Mr. Holmes. Even to me, it seems that the case against your brother is too strong to tear apart. As a famed criminologist, you must confess that the evidence is only open to one interpretation."

"I have found," said Holmes, "that interpretations can change with just a slight shift of perspective. An illusion, painstakingly created, can be revealed to be nothing more than canvas and wires if one simply walks a little to one side or the other and sees exactly how the construct is propped up. Good day to you, sir."

We followed the old man to the door. Outside, we climbed into the four-wheeler, where Holmes asked Siger, "Was your mission successful?"

"In all aspects, sir," he replied. "Even better than expected, if I may say so."

"Excellent."

"Did you get some of Morland's stationery?" asked Tenley, unaware that part of Siger's tasks included returning the bloody items to the empty outbuilding.

"Not only that," said Siger, glancing to make sure that we were far enough from Morland's house, "I found this on his desk."

He opened the knapsack, pulling out several sheets of new stationery and a soiled plain piece of cheap paper, containing a short written message. The stationery was the same as the torn and coded square that Holmes had found in Sophia's tent. The plain piece of paper, matching Sophia's supply list taken from the tent, had another similar coded message on it:

Jura pna V frr lbh? F

" 'When can I see you? S.' " said Holmes, almost instantly.

Siger nodded. " 'S' for Sophia. She even capitalized the *V* for the word *I*. To make the code less clear, they should probably only use lower-case letters, and run the words together. However, that might be a little too complicated for Sophia to manage."

"Where was this?" asked Holmes, holding up the coded sheet.

"On Morland's desk, upstairs. It was lying in a pile of other papers, bills and receipts. He had made no effort to hide it, but it wasn't lying out in an obvious way, either. I think he had simply tossed it there, and I don't think he will miss it."

"Were you seen?" asked Tenley.

"Not at all," said Siger. "Not anywhere that I went," he added, for Holmes and my benefit, I was sure, in order to let us know that he had not been observed while replacing the items in the empty outbuilding.

"The place is nearly deserted. After looking around the outbuildings, I came in through the garden. No one was around, so I went up the back stairs and searched until I located Mr. Morland's office. Finding the stationery was simple, and the message from Sophia was easily seen. After that, I came back downstairs."

Holmes held up the papers. "This is really excellent, Siger. This makes my little plan even easier to accomplish than I had originally imagined it to be."

"And what plan would that be, Mr. Holmes?" Tenley asked.

"If you would have Griffin take us back to the family home, I will give my nephew a little lesson in forgery. In the meantime, let me explain what I have in mind."

And he did. It would be something of a gamble, but it also seemed the simplest shortcut to bring this whole business to a close. I sighed, imagining yet another night, like so many before, squatting outdoors in the darkness waiting for a criminal to fall into one of Holmes's traps. At least, I thought, this time there will be no Hell Hound to deal with.

Back at the Holmes farm, Tenley asked what time he should return.

"Around ten, I expect," replied Holmes. "That will be after dark, but will still give us a couple of hours to get into position."

"I'll have my men watching earlier than that," said Tenley. "The outbuildings, you say?"

"Yes," replied Holmes. "To see if Morland visits any of them."

Tenley turned to Siger with a wry smile. "Any particular outbuilding, Siger?" he asked.

Siger looked startled. Tenley reached out and tapped the limp knapsack hanging from Siger's hand. "I won't ask what was in here," he said. "I'm not sure that I want to know at this point, and I trust Mr. Holmes. If I was really a Scotland Yard Inspector I might worry a little more about what is going on, but I'm not.

"Whatever was in this bag is not there now, and it disappeared sometime while you were searching around Morland's property. Now, you may have hidden it in the house, but since Mr. Holmes wants me to have the outbuildings watched, I'm betting it's hidden in one of them. So I ask again, just so we won't take a chance on missing it, is there any particular outbuilding that we should watch?"

Siger looked at his uncle, who appeared both pleased and amused.

Holmes nodded, and Siger replied, "The empty stable, to the west of the house." He looked down at the knapsack, and back to Tenley. "Your men should be especially aware if they see

Morland go there, and then leave the building carrying something. Perhaps a white bundle, for example."

"Very good," said Tenley, with a smile.

"Tenley," said Holmes.

"Yes, sir?"

"Do not let my brother waste your talents," said Holmes.

"Oh, he doesn't, sir. I can assure you of that. He never has." He touched the brim of his hat and turned to go.

After Tenley and Griffin departed, Holmes, Siger, and I looked at one another with expressions of amusement and relief. Then Holmes and I moved to return to the house. Siger stopped us with a question.

"What exactly was that . . . that mummified and pickled hand that was wrapped in the murdered man's robes?" he asked.

Holmes glanced at me, as if to ask how much to tell the boy. My look must have indicated to be perfectly frank, because Holmes answered with complete candor. "It is called a 'Hand of Glory.' It is an item used in the practice of black magic."

"I suspected as much," said Siger. "I knew that something like that must be used for an evil purpose. But why is such a thing in the heart of Yorkshire? What can these people believe such a thing is for?"

"No doubt it is used in dark rituals, probably the 'true path' that seems to interest Sophia so much. I suspect that it was used in the murder, giving it some sort of ceremonial flavor. Somehow, Wilkies was convinced to wear his robe and was taken to some obscure place we may not find. There, he was murdered by both Sophia and Morland, although I do not yet know if anyone else was involved, although I doubt it. Then he was placed in the pit.

"After Wilkies died and his clothing was changed to hide the ritual nature of the murder, the body was propped up in the pit, and a ceremonial slash was made across his throat, resulting in very little blood on the man's regular collar, as he was already dead at the time, and had bled out through the great wound in his back."

Siger was silent for a moment, before asking, "Where does such an item as the dead hand come from? I don't imagine one could buy something like that at just any shop in London."

Holmes replied, "These items are usually made from the dried and preserved hand of a man who has been executed, most often for murder. Usually the left, or *sinister*, hand is taken, although sometimes, if the hand is removed from a murderer, the . . . believers will try to obtain the hand that actually committed the murder.

"Occasionally the hand will be used to hold a candle, with the belief being that only the user can see the light. More extreme practitioners of the dark arts may try to make the candle from actual fat rendered from the dead man who supplied the hand. It is also believed that the possessor of such a talisman can unlock any door.

"Watson and I stumbled across a group of practitioners making use of a Hand of Glory back in the early eighties."

"What happened?" asked Siger, with wide eyes.

"They were convinced to stop using it," said Holmes, with characteristic understatement. He managed to give no indication of the danger we had both faced, and the terror and pain that we had managed to bring to an end by the violent destruction of the Black Coven. I would never forget the escape we both made though the burning house, which stood over the entrance to the coven's underground catacombs, and how we had nearly lost our lives, as well as that of the small child that I had carried up from the smoke-filled tunnels.

"That Hand of Glory is now in a museum in Walsall," Holmes added, turning toward the door. With a pat on Siger's shoulder, I followed Holmes into the house.

Inside, Holmes announced to Roberta that we would have need of the dining room for a little while. She acquiesced with a silent smile, and Holmes sent Siger off to search the house for whatever types of inks and pens he could find.

When Siger returned, he laid all the items on the table before Holmes, who had taken off his coat and rolled up his sleeves. Siger observed but did not comment on the various scars and acid marks dotting his uncle's forearms. Holmes laid out the coded messages, samples of handwriting, and blank stationery. Then, he searched among the pens and ink until he found those that most suited his purpose.

"Forgery," he said, "is an art, not a science. I can, and probably will at some point, teach you the specifics of ink types, paper qualities and manufacture, pen nibs, and so on. However, at the end of the day, the only real way to produce a forged document is to have practiced interminably beforehand, so that one knows exactly what task one's hand will be expected to perform. But also, you will need to have some sort of inborn skill, and that can never be taught, simply refined and improved. I have no doubts that you can learn the intellectual basics of the forger's business, Siger. It remains to be seen whether you have the artistic ability.

"However," he added, "we are descended from Vernet, both you and I, and that must count for something."

"Art in the blood," I muttered. Holmes thought for a moment, and then, with a sure hand, began to write a coded message on some of Morland's blank stationery. He did not write it out beforehand in order to check that he had used the correct substituted letters. Rather, he produced the final message with surety and confidence. As the letters appeared on the paper, I glanced at Morland's original message to Sophia. The writing between the two was indistinguishable.

" 'Must see you, midnight tonight, Great Rock at edge of valley forest. Urgent. M.' " Siger read, translating over his uncle's shoulder. "Do you think she will know where that is?" he asked.

"Probably," said Holmes. "It is one of the landmarks of the area, and not too far from either the campsite or Morland's house. If she does not know, she has time to find out." He blotted the paper carefully, and then said to Siger, "Can you find me a sheet of cheap paper, such as Sophia uses, so that I can construct a similar message for Mr. Morland?"

"Certainly," said Siger, dashing from the room with the enthusiasm that only a sixteen year old can produce.

I smiled at Holmes. "You are going to teach him to be a forger?" I asked. Holmes raised an eyebrow, and I said, "His mother will never forgive you."

Siger returned with several sheets of cheap paper, nearly identical to that used by Sophia. Holmes took one, thought for a moment, and then composed a similar message to Morland, signed S. After blotting it, he reached for the forged message to Morland and began to tear off the monogram at the top. Then, he stopped for a moment and handed one of the duplicate cheap sheets to Siger. "See what you can do," he said.

Siger's face took on a frown of concentration, but he showed no hesitation. He picked up the pen previously used by Holmes, pulled over the correct ink bottle, and thought for a moment, observing both the sheets with Sophia's original handwriting, and Holmes's more recent forgery. His hand moved over the blank sheet, but he did not write, not yet, as his fingers made practice swoops and lines, over and over.

Finally, he dipped his pen into the ink, lowered his hand to the paper, and wrote the coded message with confidence.

After he was done, he pushed it back, and then remembered to blot it. Then he handed it to his uncle.

Holmes examined it critically for a moment before stating, "Not bad. Not bad at all. You have captured her vowels correctly, and the narrowness of her capitals, and the down-slope of her line. However, there is too much confidence in the k's and h's, and the loops of your t's are too narrow." He dropped in onto the table. "Try again."

Siger took another blank sheet of paper, and this time, with only a moment of thought, again wrote quickly and without seeming hesitation. Blotting the message, he handed it to Holmes, who studied it intently before looking up at his anxiously watching nephew.

"Very good," he declared. "We shall send yours to Mr. Morland."

Siger nodded, and did not show much expression, but I could not miss the excitement and pride which flared just for a moment like twin lanterns deep within his gray eyes. His enthusiasm was

152

interrupted, however, when Holmes said to him, "Go get into your oldest clothes."

"Why?" Siger asked.

"Because," said Holmes, "after a suitable amount of disguise, you are going to deliver these messages to Mr. Morland and Sophia."

As Siger bounded out of the room, I shook my head, considering what Roberta's reaction would be if she discovered what Holmes had in mind for her youngest son. I decided that I would not be the one to tell her. Siger returned within moments, wearing a set of very old and tattered clothes, somewhat too small for him, with the bottom hem of his pants legs showing several inches of shin above old boots, with noticeable holes worn in the sides. Holmes stood and led Siger outside, where he proceeded to brush the lad's face and hair with dirt from the yard.

Arranging Siger's hair down over his eyes, he instructed him in the proper way to carry himself with a different posture, taking several inches off his height, and how to maintain a subservient attitude that would cause him to be ignored by most of the people that he would encounter.

"It is important," said Holmes, "for Morland to think that you have come from Wilkies's camp, while Sophia must think that you are one of Morland's stable boys. Both have met you, so it will be a challenge to make them see you as someone else. Perhaps, although I am loathe to suggest it, you might smear a little horse manure on your boots or your cuffs. That way they will be anxious for you to depart, and will pay even less attention to you."

Without hesitation, Siger stepped out, away from the house, to a mound of horse manure, in which he proceeded to muck about for a moment or two. With a grin, he returned to us, noting our involuntary expressions of distaste.

"Exactly," said Holmes. "Now let us see you walk."

Siger settled into a slouch and began to make his way back and forth across the yard. The transformation was incredible. He appeared to be nothing like the young man who had sat across from us at the dining table just a few minutes earlier. Instead, he looked like any one of the anonymous stable lads one sees and ignores everyday throughout the length of the countryside. Clearly, this boy had inherited more than just his family's deductive abilities and resemblance to his uncle. He had inborn acting talent, as well.

"Excellent," said Holmes. "Remember to seem somewhat more . . . penitent when you visit Mr. Morland. After all, you are supposed to be religious. And appear more horsey when you are at Sophia's camp. Report to us when you get back."

With that, Holmes turned and went back in. Siger, amazed that he was being trusted to do something so important with no further warnings or instructions, stood for just a moment before turning toward Morland's house.

Siger had only been gone for a few moments when a man on horseback rode up to the house. "I work with Inspector Tenley," he said. "Another cable has arrived for you, sir." Handing them to Holmes, he touched his fingers to his brow, wheeled the horse, and without a further word, turned back toward the village.

Opening the flimsy sheet, Holmes read it and then passed it to me. It simply contained more about Augustus Morland's true German background, and the name of his actual identity. "I can't see that this adds anything to helping us solve our immediate problem," I said.

"All information is useful," said Holmes.

As we walked toward the house, I said, "Didn't you once tell me that the brain is like a lumber room with limited space, and one must be careful what one takes in, so that it remains organized and does not become littered with unnecessary items, in order that something new does not crowd out something older and more useful?"

He waved his hand languidly. "I was younger then. Times and beliefs change. One must adapt or die."

Inside, Holmes seemed indisposed to talk, indicating that he wished to be alone for a while, to smoke and order his thoughts. I settled myself in a chair in the sitting room, intending to rest and think about the case. I had no sooner arranged myself,

154

however, than I stood again, walking across the room to examine several photographs that I had not previously noticed, perched on a cabinet near the window.

They were obviously old, done in the antique style used during the middle of the century. I observed one stiffly posed formal shot of a gruff man of early middle age, with a wild black beard, and the petite blonde woman beside him. Presumably these were Holmes's parents. Beside it was a small oval-shaped frame, containing a photograph of three boys.

Certainly this was of Holmes and his two older brothers. Holmes was no doubt the small fellow, only around one year of age, dressed in some sort of gown. Beside him was an already pudgy boy with extremely intelligent eyes, around eight years of age. Mycroft, I was sure. And at the right of the picture was Sherrinford, slightly older and taller, but already looking like the man he would grow to become.

There were a few other photographs of more recent origin scattered along the cabinet, all of Sherrinford, Roberta, and their three sons. I was interested to see Bancroft, the nephew that I had not yet met, and had never heard of until yesterday. He was posed in an academic gown, looking extremely intelligent, but rather haughty and proud, and already somewhat heavyset. I could see a strong resemblance to his uncle Mycroft, for whom he worked in London. "So this is the young man," I thought, "who wants to make his future without relying on the Holmes name. Bancroft Pons, indeed."

I returned to my chair, wondering when I might find something for lunch, and intending to think about the day's events and what was planned for that night. It was not long, however, before I fell asleep, that heavy afternoon sleep when the dream world and the waking world appear to merge. When the front door slammed several hours later, announcing Siger's return, I had a difficult time separating its actuality from dreamlike fantasy as I struggled to awaken.

As I rose from my chair, I heard Holmes meet Siger in the entrance hall. "How did it go?" he asked.

"Without any problems whatsoever," said Siger, with barely suppressed excitement. "They took the notes without even glancing at me, and when I mumbled about a reply, they both dismissed me. Morland either decoded his message immediately, or decided to wait until later, because he dropped the hand holding the message almost as soon as he looked at it. Sophia was hunched over when I left, puzzling through it."

"And there seemed to be no suspicion about the paper or the writing? Or about the method of delivery?"

"None at all," replied Siger. "This must have been similar to how they communicated in the past." Siger began to remove his dusty jacket.

"What do we do now?"

"We wait," said Holmes. "And hope that they simply plan to meet each other at the Great Rock tonight, without sending each other additional clarifying messages, leading to the unfortunate unraveling of our scheme."

"There is one thing that you can do, Siger," I added. Siger turned to me with an inquiring glance.

"You can take off those manure-covered boots outside before your mother sees you tracking them further into the house."

PART VII: AT THE GREAT ROCK

At a little before ten o'clock, Tenley and Griffin arrived, pulling up to the front of the house in Griffin's four-wheeler. I realized that I had never seen the man when he wasn't sitting on the driver's bench, his hands loosely holding the reins. We stepped outside and met Tenley, who had hopped down from his seat.

With us was Siger, who had informed his mother in no uncertain terms that he was coming too. We were all armed, and I could see the protests forming on Roberta's lips. However, she had held her tongue, although right before we stepped outside, she had made Siger and William promise to be careful, all the while looking at Holmes as if to make him understand that he was responsible for her sons' safety.

"Are your men in place?" Holmes asked.

Tenley nodded. "I sent some people that I trust, all with no love for Morland. They were in place soon after dark. They reported that he never went near that outbuilding. They did see him ride away for a time this afternoon, but they had no orders to follow him, so we do not know where he went." Tenley coughed, looked at the ground, and then looked back up at Holmes. "I took it upon myself to sneak into the empty stable after dark. You'll never guess what I found, Mr. Holmes. Why, it was the murdered man's robes, with the murder weapon, and something far more sinister."

"Really," said Holmes. "Well, it is fortunate indeed that it was discovered by a representative of the law, so that it can be properly taken into evidence."

"No curiosity about what else I found wrapped in the robes, Mr. Holmes?" Tenley asked with a smile.

Holmes gestured with his hand. "Time is wasting, Tenley. Perhaps we should start making our way to the Great Rock," he said, "so that we can be well concealed before our visitors arrive." We began to stroll away from the light spilling into the yard from the house windows, and into the darkened fields.

"Finding that dead hand," said Tenley, abandoning the pretense that we didn't know what he had found wrapped in the bloody robe, "puts this whole matter into a different light. It's not just a murder now, but rather some sort of diabolical execution."

"I'm sure that was how Sophia perceived it," said Holmes. "She sincerely believes that her father's form of religion was too tame, and needs to be replaced with something more evil. As for Mr. Morland, I'm not so sure. I believe that he simply used Sophia, convincing her to murder her father as a means of implicating Sherrinford so that his land grab could continue. If he hadn't found Sophia to manipulate, he would have arranged for something else to remove Sherrinford from the board."

Tenley nodded. "When he met her in Germany, back before his move to England and when he took on the Morland identity, he must have learned from her then that she disagreed with her father's teachings. At that time, he might have just spoken with her, or possibly even encouraged her, with no idea that she would be useful in the future."

"Exactly," said Holmes. "Later, when Morland was here, he decided that he needed to get rid of Sherrinford, who was an important holdout in his land purchases. Murdering him outright would cause too many problems, so he decided to have Sherrinford framed for murder instead. Having stayed in touch with Sophia, he realized that he could use her. He sent her a message and no doubt suggested that she arrange for Wilkies's group to camp here. There are certainly no old ruins or ancient sites here that would have attracted them otherwise.

"After they arrived, Morland no doubt began convincing Sophia that her father would need to be killed as a sacrifice to the 'true path,' and that Sherrinford would be the perfect man to take the blame. Sophia is obviously easily influenced, and Morland is certainly a master of manipulation. Morland has probably told Sophia that he believes the same things that she does. Possibly, he has even romanced the poor deluded girl, and she believes that he will marry her. Who knows?"

By this point, we were well away from the house, and our eyes had adjusted to the bright starlight. The fields flowed gently over rolling hillsides, and in the distance I could just make out a darkness crawling along the bottom of a low spot. This must be the valley forest, in which we planned to hide. Standing some feet out from it, shining bright in the reflected light, was a tall thin stone, fifteen to twenty feet in height. This, I was certain, was the Great Rock.

"In any event," continued Holmes, "Wilkies was ritually murdered. The weak link, of course, is Sophia, although her dogmatic stubbornness may actually keep her quiet about what was done. However, I have no doubt that at some point in the future, Morland plans to have Sophia eliminated, so that the only person who can tell the truth about what they did will be gone."

As we approached the stone, I glanced at William and Siger. William, who had been briefed by his brother earlier in the afternoon, walked forward and looked straight ahead, seemingly intent on his task. His brother, Siger, was much more alert, and his eyes darted between his forward path and Holmes. The boy listened intently to everything his uncle said, almost physically leaning toward Holmes as he walked.

"This is it," said Holmes, stopping before the tall stone. "The Great Rock. Perhaps it is not one of the old places that Wilkies traveled about to visit, but it is the closest thing that we have to it around here. Possibly Sophia will feel some sort of energy here that will make her feel like talking." Holmes glanced about. "We already have enough information on Morland to have him arrested as a spy. Now we need to get him and Sophia talking in order to have them discuss what was done to Wilkies, and so clear Sherrinford."

"Aren't you taking something of a chance with Sophia's life," I asked Holmes. "As you said, at some point Morland would probably need to eliminate her, as she is the weak link in his plan."

"I am, Watson, but I have to make that gamble. I must confess, I do not like the idea that Morland rode away this afternoon and no one knows where he went."

A figure stepped out of the nearby trees. "Everyone is hidden, sir," said Constable Worth to Tenley. "As you ordered."

"Very good," said Tenley. "I suggest that we get ourselves under cover as well." He pulled out his watch. "Ten-thirty," he said. "We must be well hidden before they arrive, especially if anyone makes early appearance to see if the place is safely deserted."

We entered the darkness of the trees, and each settled to wait in his own way. Holmes and I sat with our backs to a large tree trunk, patient as the old hunters that we were, while Siger crouched easily several feet away. William spread his coat and sat upon it cross-legged, and Tenley moved off to confer with his men.

The time passed more swiftly than it sometimes did when Holmes and I had waited in the past. The night temperature was not uncomfortable, and it was too early in the season for insects to be a problem. I could see where this low-lying growth of

159

forest might be somewhat damp at other times of the year. A few night birds called, from one part of the forest and then another. A breeze rustled the leaves overhead, but did not make enough noise to impede our attempts to hear anyone that might be approaching.

Siger occasionally shifted from side to side, but never lost the hawk-like focus that had settled on his face from the very beginning of our vigil. William, on the other hand, appeared introspective, always looking alert, but generally watching his hands, folded on the rifle lying across his knees.

As midnight approached, we all became more alert, expecting the momentary arrival of our targets. I knew that Holmes hoped that Morland and Sophia would say something incriminating to one another, especially when they realized that each had not written and sent the coded messages to the other. Hopefully, in their momentary confusion, they would make admissions that could be used against them, in order to open them up during interrogation.

I looked at my watch as midnight came, and checked it many times again over the next quarter hour, when there was no sign of any approaching visitors. Beside me, I could sense Holmes's frustration and disappointment that his stratagem had apparently failed. Finally, he signaled Tenley to draw closer, and in a whispered conference, they conceded that Morland and Sophia probably weren't coming. Siger, William, and Constable Worth joined us. After listening for a few minutes to Holmes and Tenley discuss possible options, Worth interrupted. "I think that you've been mistaken about Mr. Morland all along."

Holmes turned to him with raised eyebrows. "I concede that you have known him longer than we have," Holmes said. "What makes you think that he is not involved in this crime?"

"What would he have to gain?" asked Worth. "An important man like that, with big plans for this whole area, would not involve himself in the murder of some itinerant preacher."

"What big plans are you talking about?" asked Holmes.

"Why, the man means to bring prosperity to this corner of England," said Worth. He added, somewhat proudly, "He has discussed it with me on several occasions. It is only a matter of time until he owns all the land, creating a vast estate that he can develop into an industrial area to rival the Midlands."

"And does he have a place for you in all this?"

"Well, of course he has mentioned something of it," replied Worth. "He recognizes real talent when he sees it, and he knows the value of using a local man to police a local area."

Something in Worth's tone must have alerted Holmes. With a sharp change in his voice, Holmes asked, "How many pieces of silver did it take for you to betray us to Morland? When did you tell him that tonight was a trap?"

Worth seemed to be puzzled for a moment, as if he did not understand the question. Then he took a step back, shaking his head. "No, Mr. Holmes, you've got it all wrong. I didn't take any money."

"So you just told him as a favor between a friend to a friend?"

"No, it wasn't like that. We're not friends. He's too important to be friends with a man like me. But he respects me, and he's got important plans for this whole area. He visited me this afternoon, and he asked me how the investigation was going. I know the Inspector told me not to discuss it with Mr. Morland, so I just let him know that you and the Inspector were on the wrong track. He asked me if you were involved in a message to lure him out to the Great Rock tonight. I told him I didn't know anything about a message, but there was something being planned tonight, and that he need not inconvenience himself by coming out here at midnight."

Holmes looked at Tenley. "Inspector?"

Tenley looked into the darkness. "Holder! Jacobs! Come here!"

Two burly men appeared beside us. I hadn't heard them coming, and never saw them until they were standing there. Tenley gestured toward Worth. "Take him into custody." As the men grabbed Worth, he gave one sob and momentarily sagged toward the ground, before scrabbling his feet and trying to stand again. Tenley turned toward Holmes. "Holder and Jacobs are men that I can trust." He pulled Holmes and me aside. Siger and William followed.

"What do we do now, Mr. Holmes?" Tenley asked. "Morland is bound to be onto us."

Holmes turned back to Worth. "Constable!" he said sharply. "When you told Mr. Morland about tonight's trap, did he ask any other questions about the message used to lure him here?"

Worth ignored him, and Holmes stepped closer, raising his voice and asking the question again. One of the big men holding Worth shook him, and he finally seemed to comprehend what was being asked. "No, no he didn't. But he . . . He just said something about how the girl must have sold him out."

Holmes turned back to us. "We must get to Morland's house as quickly as possible. Tenley, how many men do you have here tonight?"

"Ten," said Tenley. "Holder and Jacobs, and eight more still out there in the dark."

"Can you trust them all?"

"Yes. I recruited them myself. They have nothing to do with Worth."

"Good. William," he said, turning to his oldest nephew. "Take four men and go to Wilkies's camp. Take Sophia into custody. Keep her there, but allow no one in to speak to her, either members of the camp, or anyone from the outside. Wait until we arrive."

William nodded, and Tenley called for the additional men still hiding in the trees to come forth. Picking four of them, William turned without a word and headed for the campsite.

Holmes said, "Holder and Jacobs. Constable Worth is under arrest. Please accompany him to the village, where he should be locked into a cell. Do not let him speak to anyone along the way. And," he added, "tell my brother that he will soon be free."

"Right, sir," said the taller of the two big men.

"Wait," said Tenley. He stepped to Worth and fished in the man's pockets, coming up with the keys to the cells. "Use these to lock up Worth, and to release Mr. Sherrinford Holmes." The big men nodded, and with little effort on their part, they began to walk the little constable between them across the fields, back toward the village.

"Right, then," said Holmes. "The rest of us, on to Morland's."

We set out at a quick pace, the eight of us, and made good time across the fields until we reached the road, where we began to increase our speed even more. There was no conversation between us, each concentrating on keeping up with Holmes, who had set a fast pace with himself out in front. Siger's long legs matched his uncle's strides. The countryside was fairly well lit by stars, in that way that is possible only in the country, where the light from the cities does not occlude the sky's visibility. Eventually, however, I began to notice a glow bleeding from behind a distant hillside. This would be Morland's house, well-lit, although it was now quite past midnight.

Reaching the house, Tenley dispersed his four men to various sides of the building, setting them in place to watch all the exits. Then we remaining four approached the front door, whereupon Holmes tried the knob, only to reveal that the door had been unlocked all along. Glancing at Tenley, who nodded to go ahead, Holmes opened the door, and we silently advanced inside.

We quickly moved from room to room, finding the ground floor abandoned. Meeting at the base of the stairs, Holmes whispered, "Siger, where is Morland's office?"

"Just upstairs, to the right," the young man replied.

"Lead on, then."

We climbed the stairs, and it did not go unnoticed by me that as we ascended, Tenley placed himself in front, taking the lead from Siger. I do not think that Siger realized what Tenley had done, so intent was he on glancing from left to right and back again, his sharp eyes missing nothing.

At the top of the stairs, Siger gestured toward a nearby doorway, lit from within and spilling light into the dark hallway. Holmes nodded and stepped to the door. I reached him as he said, "Going somewhere, Mr. Morland?"

Inside, a single desk lamp burned, revealing the thin man packing papers into a dispatch case. He looked up, more with irritation than surprise or guilt. "As a matter of fact, I have been called back to Manchester. I must leave immediately. Family business, you know."

"I don't think so," said Holmes. "You see, Sophia Wilkies has told us everything."

Siger glanced at his uncle, but showed no surprise in his face, and nothing to give away his uncle's lie. "Everything?" Morland asked. "Everything about what?"

"About the murder of her father. About how you planned it, and helped her to do it. About how you both lured him to some obscure spot in his robes, telling him it was some sort of ceremony relating to his own beliefs, and then ritually executed him. About how you changed him back to his regular clothing, propped him up in the pit, and then cut his throat."

" 'Ritually executed him' ?" repeated Morland. "Are you quite mad? I have no doubt that the girl is insane, but anything she has said that involves me is untrue. I shall have her prosecuted for slander. And you as well, I believe."

"She didn't tell us everything, of course," continued Holmes. "Not quite everything. Yet. For example, we do not know yet whether the Hand of Glory belonged to her, or if it was originally yours."

Hearing about the evil talisman used during the murder seemed to shake Morland. He did not realize that we had found it, and as far as he knew, it was still wrapped in his empty stable.

"Hand of Glory?" he said. "Don't know what you mean." He reached back toward the desk for more papers. Holmes and Siger both raised their guns higher. Seeing that, I raised mine also. "You need to step back from the desk," said Holmes. "Now," in a stronger, more commanding tone.

With a smile, Morland raised his hands and took a step backward.

"Watson?" asked Holmes. I stepped forward, taking care to stay out of my friends' line of fire, and pulled open the desk drawer for which Morland had been reaching. Inside, lying on a stack of papers, was a small, but deadly and efficient, pistol. It was obviously freshly cleaned, as gun oil had soaked and spread through the papers on which it rested.

Picking it up, I placed it in my pocket and stepped back.

"Did you wonder about the coded message from Sophia?" asked Holmes. "Would she have written it and helped to lure you into a trap if she hadn't already revealed everything to us?" he bluffed.

"Message?" asked Morland. "Do you mean that scrap of gibberish that was brought to me this afternoon by that filthy gypsy boy? Are you saying that it was a coded message from Sophia, luring me into a trap? This is quite ridiculous, Mr. Holmes. Surely if I could have understood that message, I would have gone to this meeting, thus confirming your suspicions. But since I didn't go to see her, obviously it was because I could not understand the code, which therefore confirms my innocence."

"You didn't go because Constable Worth warned you," said Holmes, noting the narrowing of Morland's eyes. "We have Worth's testimony as well. You really are caught, you know," he added. "We have even retrieved the dead man's robes and what was contained within them from where you hid them in your stalls." Morland said nothing for a moment. He did not even allow any expression to pass across his face. Finally, he said, with just a possibility of tentativeness in his voice, "Robes? In my stalls? I don't know what you're talking about. If you found anything in my out-buildings, it must have been placed there by someone else. Possibly this mad Sophia put it there, or one of her people. Maybe that filthy boy that delivered the message did it."

"This is the 'filthy boy,' " said Tenley, nodding his head toward Siger. "He brought the message to you. You're not as smart as you think. You didn't even take a good look at who he was."

"You are the one who is not very smart, Inspector," said Morland. "You have burst into my house, held me at gunpoint, and detained me from my lawful activities, based on the ridiculous story of some crazy girl who apparently murdered her father, and has since tried to mask her own guilt by spreading it around onto her betters! I'm soon to be a peer of the realm. I cannot be treated this way!"

165

"Peer of the realm?" said Holmes. "It won't do, *Mr.* Morland. It really won't. Or perhaps I should address you as *Baron Ennesfred Kroll*!" Morland stepped back, and seemed to sag for just a moment before pulling himself back up. His eyes widened, and he moved his mouth as if to speak, but nothing came forth.

"We really do know it all, Baron Kroll," said Holmes. "We know about your true identity, and how you assumed that of the real Morland more than twenty years ago, following his death in Germany. We know how you took over the family fortune, estates, and title following the death of Morland's father, and how you ran the Morland business from Germany.

"We know about how you met Sophia when she was in Germany, and learned of her fascination with the Satanic religions, something her father never would have tolerated. We know how you finally returned to this country, and began buying lands to create a vast unobserved area on the northeast coast of England, which could be used at some point in the future as a sort of secret German colony, for troops and supplies to be assembled and organized under cover, should an invasion ever occur.

"Finally, we know how my brother was a hold-out to your plan, refusing to sell his large and centrally located estate. It wasn't supposed to happen that way, was it, Baron Kroll? All of the land owners were supposed to be easily swayed by your offers and your seeming infinite financial resources, backed by the very German treasury itself. We know how you manipulated Sophia into convincing her father to come to this area, and finally how you helped her to murder him, using the iron dagger, with its oddly Germanic markings, and the hideous dead man's Hand of Glory.

"As you can see, Baron Kroll, we know it all. And we have known it for quite a while. There is an old saying about giving a man enough rope to hang himself. Do you have such a saying in Germany? Well, you were being given rope, and far earlier than was expected, you hung yourself by becoming involved in a murder."

166

The sound of footsteps came up the stairs and then down the short hallway. William stepped into the room, breathing hard. I knew that he was supposed to stay with Sophia, and wondered what could have happened to make him come here instead.

"Well?" asked Holmes.

"She was dead," replied William. "In her tent. Throat cut. None of those people heard or saw anything. Or so they say."

Holmes cursed and met my eyes. We both knew where Morland had gone this afternoon when no one followed him. I was aware that Holmes would hold himself responsible for allowing the girl's death to occur. Morland, or Baron Kroll, as I would have to think of him now, smiled and said, "I believe that without a witness, any attempt to link me to this murder will be doomed to failure." He stepped forward. "Now, as I said, Inspector, I must be leaving on family business. I do not know what this foolishness is about me being a German citizen, but I can assure you that if you do not stand aside, I will make sure that you yourself are brought up on charges. Do I make myself clear?"

Tenley smiled. "You don't seriously think I'm going to let you walk out of here, do you, Baron Kroll? Because I — "

Before he could finish, Kroll had pivoted and dropped, reaching for a lower drawer on his desk. Pulling it open, he rose in one fluid movement, holding another pistol, and swinging it up. From my position, I could not tell where he intended to aim it, and I could not see whether his finger was tightening as he prepared to fire. In any case, I considered the man to be as dangerous as a mad dog, and I had no hesitation whatsoever.

I fired twice. The first bullet passed through Kroll's upraised wrist, causing the gun to spin and sag on his forefinger before dropping to the floor. The sound of it hitting the wood was unheard as it was drowned out by my second shot, the bullet flying true into Baron Kroll's knee. As he turned to me in shock, and started to sag to the ground, I stepped forward, kicking him to one side as I knocked his fallen gun to the other.

"Well done, Dr. Watson!" cried Siger. "Oh, well done!"

167

I cleared my throat. "Holmes usually prefers to avoid this type of conclusion to his cases," I said. "However, I suspect that if I had allowed this madman to shoot either of her children, or even her brother-in-law, Roberta Holmes would have shot me as well, and I did not travel all the way to Yorkshire in order to make such fine new friends, only to have to turn around and bury some of them."

PART VIII: A FAMILY REUNITED

When we arrived at the village cells, Holmes paused for a moment in front, staring up at the tall structure. "You say this oversized building was financed and built by Sir Clive Owenby?" he asked.

Tenley regarded him with a smile. "Yes," he replied. "Sir Clive lives in York."

"I believe that you stated that he is a crony of my brother Mycroft's," said Holmes.

"They are somewhat acquainted," confirmed Tenley. "Is it important?"

"I theorize," said Holmes, "that the idea behind this building's construction lies along the same lines of thinking as Baron Kroll's attempts to create a pocket German fiefdom here in Yorkshire. This building is intended to remain here, looking simply like the location of an oversize village constabulary, until such time as it might be needed. Sir Clive, at my brother's urging, has financed this inconspicuous fortress. No doubt there are some interesting secrets inside, possibly an unknown cellar, or cellars. And perhaps some of the Queen's weapons stored in them as well, in case the citizens might someday need to be armed at short notice against German invaders?"

Tenley looked to make sure that Kroll was a considerable distance away. "I won't confirm anything specific, Mr. Holmes, but I will say that whatever secrets that building does contain, they are well hidden and there is no way Constable Worth of any of his ilk ever suspected anything, and certainly no way that the Germans could know about it."

Upstairs, we found Sherrinford talking with Holder and Jacobs, while Constable Worth sat on the cot in his locked cell, his head resting in his hands. Outside in the hall, Baron Kroll was surrounded by all of Tenley's remaining men and Dr. Dalton, who had been summoned to treat Kroll's wounds. Kroll was nearly completely hidden within the cluster of angry Yorkshiremen and one grim doctor. Sherrinford stepped forward, embracing his two sons, and then grabbing Holmes in a bear hug, before releasing him and shaking his hand. Then he turned toward me. I stepped forward, my hand outstretched, but he bypassed it, hugging me as well. After releasing me, he turned back to Tenley. "Worth hasn't said a word since he got here," he said. "Holder and Jacobs let me know what he did. What has happened since they brought him here?"

We related to Sherrinford the confrontation at the Morland house, and William's subsequent revelation that Sophia had been murdered. Worth moaned to himself. Upon hearing of the girl's violent death, Sherrinford leaned to one side, looking into the hall as if to get a glimpse of Kroll. He was unable to see him, however, due to the fact that the German was blocked by the big country men surrounding him.

"I think that we shall have to release Worth on his own recognizance," said Holmes, to our surprise.

"Why, Mr. Holmes?" asked Tenley. "If we leave them together, we might overhear some incriminating conversation."

"True," replied Holmes. "However, Baron Kroll is going to be a very different kind of prisoner, and we would do well to keep him entirely separated from Worth. The murders of Wilkies and his daughter are simply a small part of the bigger picture. This man is a German agent. Mycroft may or may not decide that it is more effective for Kroll to disappear into a prison somewhere, leaving the Germans in disarray and confusion regarding their land-grab plan and the disappearance of their man. Or it may be decided to try Kroll as Augustus Morland for the murders, but limit information from the trial that is released to the public. In any case, we need to keep Kroll separate from everyone that we can from this moment on.

"I'm sure," he added, glancing at Worth, "that this man can be released without any risk of flight. After all, only a few of us here know about his involvement. He is a ruined and broken man, and I'm certain that he knows what's good for him. He will not be the type to talk about these events, which put him in such a bad light. I'm certain that we can count on his discretion."

Worth, who had apparently been listening despite his attitude of despair, jumped up. "Oh, I promise, sirs!" he cried. "I won't say anything. I have learned my lesson."

"Of course," Holmes went on, conversationally, "you have resigned your position as constable, effective immediately, and you will be observed closely for a long time to come." Worth stared at him, seeing that his freedom was not going to come without some cost, after all. He swallowed once or twice, and then said, in a much quieter and emotionless voice, "Yes, sir. Of course. I understand."

Worth's cell was soon unlocked, and he was led by one of his big guards — I never did know which was Holder and which was Jacobs — out past the group of men in the hall, making sure that he was allowed no contact whatsoever with Kroll. After he had gone, Kroll was placed in a center cell. Holmes remained behind for a moment, staring wordlessly at the prisoner, who returned his gaze with venomous hate.

Then Holmes joined us in the hall, leaving the German under guard by several of our night's companions. Downstairs, Tenley emphasized to the remaining men the need to keep the entire affair secret, no matter what version of events that they might hear in the next few days. The men, all good British citizens, agreed and departed.

"I will cable London and your brother with the details," said Tenley. "You get Mr. Sherrinford Holmes here back to his family."

He shook hands with all of us, and went back inside. I looked around, and saw, sitting off to the side of the building, Griffin. He was on the driver's seat, as usual, with no indication that he wanted to be anywhere else, in spite of the fact that it was after three in the morning. Stepping over to him, I asked whether he

170

could take us back to the Holmes farm. Without a word, he nodded. In a moment, the five of us were on board and the short trip began.

Roberta was still up when we arrived. Her joy at seeing the safe return of her husband and two sons was palpable. She would not rest until she heard the whole story. We had to repeatedly decline her offer to make a full meal right then instead of waiting for breakfast. Finally, as the sky began to lighten with the coming dawn, we made our way to bed in order to catch a few hours of sleep. All of us, that is, except Holmes and Siger.

If Siger was like his uncle, he did not need much sleep in any case, so I doubt if staying up the rest of the night seriously tired either of them. To this day, I do not know what they talked about, although I am fairly certain that the discussion probably included an examination of the minute details of the recent events. I also believe that they discussed Siger's chosen future.

I do know that later that year, Siger entered Oxford at the young age of sixteen. His intellect was a deciding factor, but possibly the influence of his uncles helped as well. A few years later, in 1899, Siger graduated and immediately approached his uncle, asking Holmes to allow Siger to become something of an apprentice, learning the varied skills needed by a consulting detective. At that time, I was still living in Baker Street, and I had been prohibited by Holmes from publishing any more of his cases. Holmes knew that I still kept extensive notes on his investigations, however, and he instructed me that I was never to mention Siger in any of them, most likely because he wanted to spare Siger from gaining a reputation based upon appearances in a popular publication.

In October 1903, Holmes was faced with an unexpected crisis in the form of the sudden death of Irene Adler. I have never mentioned in any published accounts the regard Holmes had always felt for Irene, who had been widowed by Godfrey Norton in late 1890. The following year she had given birth to Godfrey's daughter, and had resumed her career on the operatic stage. Holmes had become reacquainted with her soon after his supposed disappearance at the Reichenbach Falls. In 1892, she gave birth to a son, Scott. After Holmes's return to England in 1894, we had infrequent contact with her. Her fortunes went into decline, and in the late 1890's she married a wealthy man who subsequently died.

Several more meetings between Irene, Holmes, and myself took place over the next few years. Eventually Irene moved with her family to Montenegro, a location that seemed to hold some sentimental attachment for her. In 1901, she married her third husband, a man named Vukcic, which loosely translates to "little wolf." Vukcic had a son of his own. Irene remained in Montenegro until her untimely death.

I had initially believed Irene Adler was something of an adventuress, based upon the original description of her by the King of Bohemia, but as I came to know her in later years, I realized that she was a lady of high morals who had been much maligned by the king. As this document which I am preparing will be placed with my other records at the Cox and Company Bank for at least seventy-five years after my death, I feel that I can elaborate on what happened after Irene's death, and how those events relate to Siger, without bringing any negative reflection on the lady.

I will never forget that October 1903, when I received Holmes's request to visit his rooms in Baker Street. I had remarried by then, and was living several streets away in Queen Anne Street, where I had resumed my private medical practice. I found Holmes smoking in his chair before his fire. Littering the floor of the sitting room were several packing boxes. "Going somewhere?" I asked Holmes.

"I have decided to retire."

Before I could process this odd and unexpected statement, for Holmes was only forty-nine years old at the time, Holmes handed me the telegram, containing the details of Irene's death in a railway accident. The implications washed over me. Some were obvious, and some I was not supposed to know but had figured out for myself.

"What about her son and daughter?" I asked.

"They are all right," said Holmes. "Her daughter wishes to remain in Montenegro. Her son . . . . He will be here in a few days." He paused for a second, and said, "Watson, there is something that I must tell you about the boy." He shifted in his seat, looking uncomfortable, one of the few times I have ever seen him so. The time he had apologized to me after making me believe that he had been poisoned by Culverton Smith. The time that he had returned from a three-year absence, leaving me to believe that he was dead, while only his brother Mycroft had known the truth. A few others as well. I saw no reason to extend his discomfort.

"I already know, Holmes." He didn't look up. "I know that he is your son."

We were silent for a moment, and he did not ask how that I knew. We never discussed it again, and to this day I do not know the details. Nor do I want to. After a moment, he began to speak. He told me how he had been spending more and more time of late working on matters for his brother Mycroft, especially relating to Britain's relations with the rest of the world, and specifically Germany. For a year or more, Mycroft had been pressuring him to become something of a full-time agent for the shadowy secret department that Mycroft controlled, as the certainty of war with Germany loomed ever closer. The arrival of the boy would allow Holmes to do as Mycroft wished, in a limited way.

He intended to announce his retirement immediately, and depart to live near Beachy Head in Sussex, in a small coastal cottage that he had acquired several years earlier, during the course of an investigation. He intended to maintain the Baker Street rooms, however, as a retreat while in London. Mrs. Hudson had agreed to move to Sussex with him, to help care for the boy. And he was going to keep bees.

In order to complete the illusion of Holmes's retirement, I would begin to publish accounts of his cases once again in *The Strand* magazine, which had been approached by the government and was more than willing to help, considering the financial windfall they would be reaping. My old friend and literary agent,

173

Conan Doyle, had already been briefed and was willing to help. The first published case would be *The Empty House,* relating Holmes's return to life in 1894. And I must specifically include a statement that Holmes had retired, and that it was only due to that reason that I was allowed to resume publication of the stories.

And so, within a day or so, Holmes had ensconced himself in Sussex. Soon after that, Scott Adler Holmes arrived at his father's new home.

I was there when the precocious eleven-year-old greeted his father.

They had met several times over the years, but I never knew if Scott realized before his mother's death and the subsequent reading of her will that Holmes was his father. Mrs. Hudson bustled around and made the boy feel at home, and I did my best to welcome him as well. However, I do not think that anyone comforted him more during that time than did his cousin, Siger Holmes.

At that time, Siger had trained with Holmes for several years, one of several apprentices that Holmes had taken on during the early years of the century. Siger's activities had transitioned gradually from those of a consulting detective to that of an agent, working for his uncle Mycroft and brother Bancroft, now himself quite a rising figure within the British government. Siger had been on hand during Holmes's move to Sussex.

At that time, he was twenty-three years of age, tall and lean, and looked almost exactly like his uncle Sherlock. He still retained much of his boyish enthusiasm, however, and I believe that was what bonded him to Scott Holmes.

The young boy adapted well. He met Mycroft and Bancroft a few days after his arrival, and I went with them all to Yorkshire in November, where Scott was welcomed by the rest of his new family. It warmed my heart to see how Roberta mothered the boy, immediately surrounding him with the unconditional love with which she had filled her home and had raised three fine sons. In later years, while Holmes was off continuing his investigations, Scott would spend a great deal of time in

174

Yorkshire, and Roberta would become like a second mother to him, as she had been to his father as well.

That November was the last time that the Holmes family, with myself included as a sort of adopted uncle and brother, would all be together in one place. In later years, with the War approaching, the family would be scattered, and there was never a chance to assemble the entire group again.

As Scott grew, his friendship with Siger grew as well. Siger nicknamed the boy "Caesar" due to Scott's assured bearing and attitude.

By this point, Scott was showing the same deductive skills as evidenced by the rest of his family. In 1907, Siger opened his own practice as a consulting detective, finding increasing success over the course of several years. However, he was dismayed that many people came to him expecting the services of his uncle Sherlock, based upon the name Holmes. He began to see why his brother Bancroft had taken a different last name.

In 1911, Scott inadvertently became involved in a series of events that resulted in the defeat of a group that would have prevented the crowning of King George V. By that time, the nineteen-year-old young man had eschewed college, preferring to educate himself, learning more that way than he probably could have by attending any university. As a result of Scott's service to the Crown, he was officially recruited into Mycroft Holmes's organization, where he and Siger became a team that was unparalleled for its masterful successes in discovering information to aid the British government as the threat of war rolled ever closer.

Working together, the two young men criss-crossed Europe. Siger often used the name "Mr. Bridges," an Anglicization of his brother's assumed last name, *Pons*. Scott would usually go by his nickname, Caesar, or other names of Roman leaders, combined with variants of the word *wolf* as a surname. Their exploits and antics during this time became something of a legend, and although they frequently vexed Mycroft Holmes and Bancroft Pons to no end, no one could argue with their results.

175

This continued, of course, until the Great War began. I was staying with Holmes in Sussex in late August of that year, 1914, when Siger came to see his uncle. Both realized that their conversation might be the last quiet visit they would have for some time. Holmes had recently returned from a two-and-a-half-year absence, traveling the United States and Great Britain as "Altamont," the renegade Irishman and German agent. His masterful impersonation had ended only a few weeks before, with the arrest of the sinister von Bork.

Siger stated that after the war, he wished to resume his private practice, but he would like to make his own name, and not rest on his uncle's reputation, as had been the earlier problem. He seemed to be asking for some sort of permission from Holmes to step away from the family name. Holmes suggested that Siger use an alias, based on Siger's previous preference for "Mr. Bridges" and also his brother Bancroft's changed surname at the Foreign Office. They experimented with several variations before Holmes suggested something appealing, recalling a comment made by Holmes at the end of the Yorkshire investigation in June 1896. Siger decided that he would adopt the name suggested to him by Sherlock Holmes: *Solar Pons.*

Of course, that was years in the future. Little did Holmes and Siger know, during that early morning conversation in Yorkshire while the rest of the family slept, what was ahead of all of us on our long road. The successes and tragedies were all hidden from us then, as well as the fact that Baron Ennesfred Kroll would escape from British custody in October of that same year, only to resume his true identity and vex Siger in later years, much as Professor Moriarty had plagued Holmes.

I arose late that morning, and was dismayed and embarrassed to see my watch indicating that the morning was nearly gone. I dressed hurriedly and went downstairs, where Roberta did her best to make me feel as if my long slumber was the most natural thing in the world. She and Sherrinford, along with William, had been up since daybreak, taking care of the daily work, while

Holmes and Siger had gone back to the village to check on the prisoner.

Later that morning, I was just finishing my belated breakfast when a commotion arose out in the yard. Roberta leaned in and said, "You'd better come out, Dr. Watson."

Stepping into the sunshine, I saw several men descending from Griffin's sturdy four-wheeler. As my eyes adjusted to the light, I saw Holmes and Siger, followed by the heavier and more awkward figures of Mycroft Holmes and a similar looking younger fellow who could only be Bancroft.

Sherrinford and Roberta greeted their prodigal son, while William and Siger grinned. Mycroft nodded in my direction, and when Bancroft was free, he stepped over and introduced himself.

"Bancroft Pons, doctor. A pleasure to meet you."

"The pleasure is all mine," I said, shaking his hand.

"Bancroft *Holmes*," said his mother. "You are home now. That other silly name can remain in London."

"As you like," replied Bancroft.

We went inside, where Roberta bustled about, serving refreshments. I was not very hungry, having just eaten, but I did manage to put away at least one serving of a delicious yellow cake. As I was eating, discussions moved quickly around the table, as everyone was caught up on the events of the last few days. Mycroft and Bancroft explained that they had arranged a special train to leave London as soon as they had received Tenley's wire, explaining the details of Baron Kroll's arrest.

"I understand you were quite helpful, brother," said Bancroft to Siger.

"He was truly a bridge of sunlight throughout the whole affair," said Holmes, causing his youngest nephew to puff up in a most comical way with pride.

Bancroft snorted. "A bridge of sunlight, indeed! If only you could approach your studies with the same solar intensity that you have shown relating to your desire to become a detective."

"By the way, Watson," Holmes said, changing the subject, "Baron Kroll tried to kill himself last night."

I raised my eyebrows. "Really? How?"

"His guards thought he was asleep, and he tried to fashion a noose from a bed sheet. He was caught, however, and his attempt was prevented."

"Just as well, I suppose," said Mycroft. "We will have to let him go, eventually, but not before we get all the use out of him that we can."

Baron Kroll ended up staying in the village lock-up for several months, during which time he was closely interrogated by Tenley and other individuals sent up from London. He was not moved to a larger prison in order to preserve the security of his arrest. Before he could be officially sent back to Germany, he escaped.

Mycroft shifted his big frame in the small chair. "Baron Kroll does seem to have conceived an intense dislike for the Holmes name."

"And the Pons name, as well," added Bancroft. "After we identified ourselves, I could see him committing it to memory with the same hatred that he was showing towards you, uncle."

"Pons, Pons," cried Roberta. "I wish you'd never decided to use that name."

"Actually, the boy comes by it honestly," said Sherrinford, speaking for the first time. He had been looking with quiet fondness from one member of his family to another since we had come inside.

"How do you mean?" asked Siger.

"He is not the first to use that alias," replied Sherrinford. "I myself used it, a few years back."

Roberta and Mycroft both looked at him suddenly, their glances filled with similar warnings. Sherrinford continued as if he did not notice.

"William probably remembers some of this, and I know Bancroft is aware of the details, but you have never heard this story, Siger. Back in 1880, just before you were born, I did a little favor for your uncle Mycroft."

Siger sat up straight, eyes alert. I glanced at Holmes, and could tell that he had never heard this tale, either. "Without getting into many specifics," Sherrinford continued, "I was asked to travel to Prague, where I carried out a mission for Her Majesty's government, delivering a message to the Bohemian royal family. In order to hide my activities, I traveled with my family. William was only nine, and Bancroft was about seven. And your mother was very much burdened with you at that point Siger, since this was right before the time of your birth."

"A mad time to make me travel," muttered Roberta. "Although I will admit that Prague was a lovely city . . . ."

"In any case," said Sherrinford, "I carried out my mission, although I must say that sort of intrigue is not to my liking. I am happy to leave it to those who enjoy it. While we were there in Prague, Siger, you were born."

"I did not know that," said Siger softly.

"Neither did I," said Holmes. "As I recall, I visited Yorkshire a month or so after Siger's birth, and you were all here at home as if you had never left, and no one mentioned a thing to me at all about a trip to Prague."

"I'm sure you understand the nature of security, Sherlock," interrupted Mycroft, "As do you, Sherrinford. I think that this discussion should be concluded."

"Strange," continued Holmes, ignoring Mycroft, "when I met the King of Bohemia, he never mentioned having previously met my brother."

"He didn't know me as your brother, you see," replied Sherrinford. "Hence my previous use of the name *Pons*. When I traveled there, I went under the identity of Asenath Pons, a visiting consular official. Years later, when Bancroft went to work for Mycroft, he must have read the file and taken the name Pons as well, for his own reasons."

"And I always thought you came up with it on your own," said Siger to his brother, who did not comment.

"As did I, said Holmes. "I understand the derivation of the name Pons from your name, Sherrinford, but I wonder if mad old cousin Asenath would appreciate that you appropriated *his* name for your role?

"He will never hear about it," grinned Sherrinford. "Security, you know."

Mycroft interrupted at that point, urging that all discussion of the matter be dropped. Siger and Bancroft joined in as well, with Holmes and Sherrinford offering their opinions, and in a moment, even William was participating. I watched them, two generations of Holmes brothers, the air in the room nearly popping with the electricity being generated by their combined personalities and intellects. I became aware of Roberta, sitting beside me and watching them as well, her lovely face beaming with pride.

"They are something wonderful, are they not, doctor?" she said, very softly.

"Indeed," I replied. "And you have made a wonderful home for them here."

"Thank you," she said. Then turning slightly toward me, she said, "You must consider this your home, and yourself a part of this family, as well."

Her earnest gaze stopped any polite refusal that might have initially risen to my lips. I glanced back at the group of men, all arguing and teasing each other in a good-natured way. I realized that I would be very happy, indeed, to be included in such a group.

"Thank you," I said to her. "It pleases me very much to be a part of your family."

She patted my arm and turned back to look at the men surrounding the table. I realized that I was hungrier than I thought, and reached to cut another piece of cake.

Postscript: Two Letters*

9 July, 1929

Dear Willie,

I hope that this letter finds you and your family in excellent health, and that you are doing well. I apologize for not having written in so long, and can only beg your forgiveness and understanding. I could plead that the long intervals between letters is due to my age, but I must confess that I have been writing, working on more records of Holmes's cases, so I really have no good excuse at all.

I was sorry to hear of your mother's passing, as well as the tragic death of your young son Howard from rabies. I realize that it has been two years since they both passed, but I know that you must still think of them every day. I am greatly saddened that in this modern world in which we live, a treatable disease such as rabies was still able to take your son from you.

As I mentioned, I have been working to complete a number of my records of Holmes's cases, and recently I came across the notes I made during our visit to your part of the world in 1921. Although it was just a few short years ago, I must confess that it seems like much longer, as my age has really caught up with me in the intervening years. Upon completion of the manuscript, I propose to send you a copy, with the fond hope that you and your family might enjoy a record of those two days.

Holmes and I have stayed busy since that time, although I must admit that Holmes has been more active than I. He has still engaged himself in the occasional investigation, while I am more content to remain in England. However, he and I both traveled to your country in the fall of 1927, where we were involved in one of the most trying matters of our careers.

---

* EDITOR'S NOTE: These are the letters that were folded in the back of the composition book found in my aunt's belongings . . .

Before the case was over, we had asked several people to come over from London to help us, including Holmes's nephew and a former Belgian policeman, both of whom have set up private consulting detective practices in London. Joining Holmes's nephew was his good friend, Dr. Parker. In New York, we were assisted by Holmes's son — now there's a fellow you didn't know about, I'll wager! — as well as his assistant, a Mr. Goodwin, and also the unlikely team of one of the New York Police inspectors and his brilliant son, Ellery, who shows every sign of being Holmes's deductive rival.

In spite of the fact that we had all of that deductive brain power working on the case, I don't think that the matter could have been satisfactorily concluded without the last minute arrival of a young law student from California named Mason, who provided the last bit of missing and vital information to our case.

After the matter concluded, we had a wonderful celebration at the Hotel Algonquin, before those of us returning to England all set sail together. (Of course, I know that I don't have to ask you to keep this information to yourself, as the identity of both Holmes's son and his nephew are both rather closely guarded secrets.)

Since that time, I have lived a relatively peaceful life, working, as I said, on putting my notes in order. However, I was excited to hear from Holmes just the other day. He needs my help on another case! It seems that his son, who has been living in New York for several years and working as a private detective under some outlandish assumed name, has traveled to Zagreb to track down the whereabouts of a girl, Anna, that he adopted in 1921, during the time he wandered Europe after the War. Now he has been thrown into jail there, and we are off to rescue him! Joining us will be Holmes's nephew and Dr. Parker.

While I am traveling, I will continue to work on the manuscript of our Tennessee visit, along with a few others, and will forward to you a completed version when I return to England. In the meantime, I hope that everything is going well for you and yours, and that I will be able to visit the United

States again at some point in the future, where we will be able to renew our friendship in person.

Until that time, remember that I am,

Always your friend (and distant cousin!),

John H. Watson

* * * * * *

8 August, 1929

Dear Mr. Marcum,

I am very sad to inform you that Watson passed away on 24 July of pneumonia, which he acquired while traveling with me and some associates to Zagreb on something of a rescue mission. I knew that Watson's health had been failing for some time, but against my better judgment, I allowed him to accompany us. It thrilled him, I believe, to be asked to go along on one more investigation.

He became ill on the way back from our journey, which I can tell you was a complete success. I insisted that he return with me to my Sussex home to recuperate, but after we had settled in there, his condition worsened, and he died peacefully a few days later.

As the enclosed letter from Watson mentions, he had worked for the past several years on the monumental task of wrestling his voluminous notes into some sort of readable shape. He had completed a number of manuscripts, some of which have been place in safe-keeping, while others he generously gave to the individuals involved in the events that he had recorded.

He had finished preparing the narrative of our trip to your part of the world, as well as a few other stories contained in the same copy book, when he died. I have kept his final versions of the events, but I thought, as it was his intention to send you a copy of the narrative, that you might like to have the original copy book, containing a few other matters as well.

It may interest you to read that after we left you in Rockwood that day, we journeyed back to Knoxville, and then on to Maryville, where we were able to stop a rather diabolical assembly. During that time, we had a chance to spend several days in and around Maryville College. I believe that Watson has mentioned to me how you attended this college for a few years in 1911 or 1912. Possibly you will recognize some place where you walked there as you read Watson's narrative.

Watson and I both enjoyed meeting you, and Watson was very proud of his American cousins. If there is ever anything that I can do for you, do not hesitate to let me know.

With all best wishes,

SHERLOCK HOLMES

About the Editor

David Marcum began his study of the lives of Sherlock Holmes and Dr. Watson as a boy in 1975 when, while trading with a friend to obtain Hardy Boys books, he received an abridged copy of *The Adventures of Sherlock Holmes*, thrown in as a last-minute and little-welcomed addition to the trade. Soon after, he saw *A Study in Terror* on television and began to search out other Holmes stories, both Canon and pastiche. He borrowed way ahead on his allowance and bought a copy of the Doubleday edition of *The Complete Sherlock Holmes* and started to discover the rest of the Canon that night. His parents gave him Baring-Gould's *Sherlock Holmes of Baker Street* for Christmas and his fate was sealed.

Since that time, he has been reading and collecting literally thousands of Holmes's cases in the form of short stories, novels, movies, radio and television episodes, scripts, comic books, unpublished manuscripts, and fan-fiction. In addition, he reads mysteries by numerous other authors, including those that he considers the classics, Nero Wolfe, Ellery Queen, Hercule Poirot, Perry Mason, and Holmes's logical heir, Solar Pons.

When not immersed in the activities of his childhood heroes, David is employed as a licensed civil engineer. He lives in Tennessee with his wife and son, and plans with great passion to finally travel one day to Baker Street in London, the location he most wants to visit in the whole world.

Questions and comments may be addressed to:

thepapersofsherlockholmes@gmail.com

Also from MX Publishing

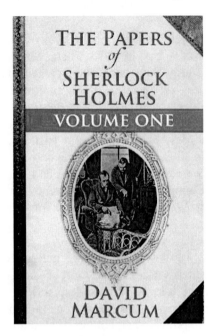

The Papers of Sherlock Holmes Volume I

More traditional Sherlock Holmes stories from David Marcum

IN PREPARATION:
Sherlock Holmes and A Quantity of Debt

MX Publishing is the world's leading Sherlock Holmes books publisher with over 100 titles.

www.mxpublishing.com

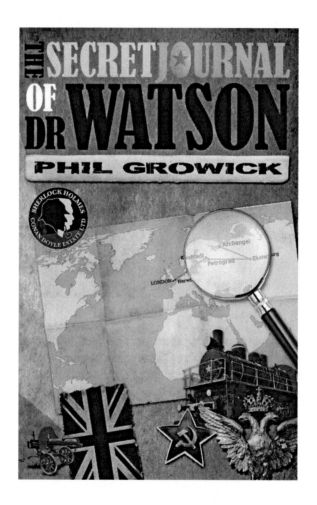

The Secret Journal of Dr Watson

www.mxpublishing.com

Also from MX Publishing

Winners of the 2011 Howlett Literary Award (Sherlock Holmes
book of the year) for 'The Norwood Author'

From the world's largest Sherlock Holmes publishers dozens of
new novels from the top Holmes authors.
www.mxpublishing.com

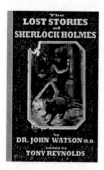 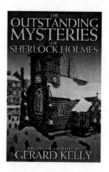

Including our bestselling short story collections 'Lost Stories of
Sherlock Holmes' , 'The Outstanding Mysteries of Sherlock
Holmes', 'Untold Adventures of Sherlock Holmes' (and the
sequel 'Studies in Legacy) and 'Sherlock Holmes in Pursuit'.

Also from MX Publishing

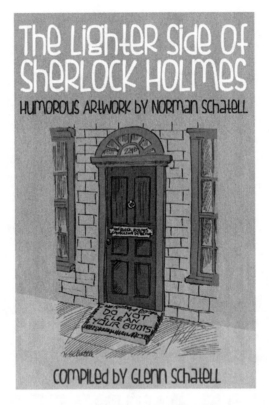

In paperback and hardback, 300 wonderful Holmes cartoons.

www.mxpublishing.com

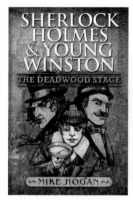  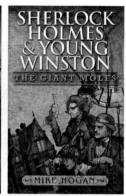

Audio Books

www.audiogo.co.uk

 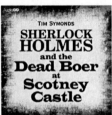 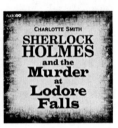

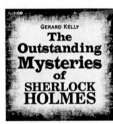  

Links

The Publishers support the Save Undershaw campaign – the campaign to save and restore Sir Arthur Conan Doyle's former home. Undershaw is where he brought Sherlock Holmes back to life, and should be preserved for future generations of Holmes fans.

Save Undershaw   www.saveundershaw.com

Sherlockology   www.sherlockology.com

MX Publishing   www.mxpublishing.com

You can read more about Sir Arthur Conan Doyle and Undershaw in Alistair Duncan's book (share of royalties to the Undershaw Preservation Trust) – An Entirely New Country and in the amazing compilation Sherlock's Home – The Empty House (all royalties to the Trust).

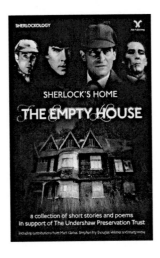

193